KEEPING GLORIA SWANSON

Keeping Gloria Swanson

A novel
by

MARK ALBRO

Adelaide Books
New York / Lisbon
2019

KEEPING GLORIA SWANSON
A novel
By Mark Albro

Copyright © by Mark Albro
Cover design © 2019 Adelaide Books

Published by Adelaide Books, New York / Lisbon
adelaidebooks.org
Editor-in-Chief
Stevan V. Nikolic

For any information, please address Adelaide Books
at info@adelaidebooks.org
or write to:
Adelaide Books
244 Fifth Ave. Suite D27
New York, NY, 10001

ISBN-10: 1-950437-53-1
ISBN-13: 978-1-950437-53-5

Printed in the United States of America

For Josh

"My mother and I could always look out the same window

without ever seeing the same thing."

Gloria Swanson

1

I want my story to begin with a 3-D urban twist on the opening shots of *The Sound of Music*: handsome me twirling in an explosion of Parisian summer beauty, sunshine and surround-sound music, perhaps the opening lines of France Gall's iconic "*Laisse tomber les filles*," – so hyperbolically cool, her perky tits against a 60's shiny blouse (can I say that or is it retro-harassment? #vintagemetoo) – Paris draped along the Seine, the spidery Pont des Arts (choked with tourists, though no longer padlocking a token of their porcine love on the fret work), the stoutly proud Pont Neuf, the elegant Pont Louis Philippe, the bridge connecting the Ile St. Louis to the *Quai de l'Hôtel de Ville*: sunny afternoon Paris, Berthillon ice cream, and the sassy accompaniment of France Gall (tits or no tits). But that's how I *wish* my story began. In fact, I yearn for that *to be* my story; I'd love to be living in a Maxfield Parrish version of Paris, instead of a neurotic metropolis with air pollution alerts, lackadaisical soldiers, sharp-tongued store clerks, and a sweaty reek of fear in the air (a primordial fug, wafting from the top of shirts and blouses).

Some of my story – in its general design – begins anew whenever I dive under the bed, where I keep a blanket and pillow that I wash once a week on Wednesday. Often, that doesn't work, and I need to slither out and curl up in the corner of the wardrobe in the guest room (it's enormous that wardrobe), hiding behind old overcoats, sobbing and peeing in my work slacks, until I sleep – only waking when I snore too loudly or our *femme de ménage* finds me and shifts me onward. She has that indomitable cheery spirit of most Portuguese workers in Paris. Occasionally, Théophile opens the door, and I tumble out on his feet. He merely shrugs and says, "I don't suppose you phoned in ill?" It's France; I don't need to; they know my problem. Nobody cares. They give lip service, of course, but they care more about their dinner, as they should. Somebody else's trauma is roadkill on a day's adventure; who needs that? People make clucking sorrowful noises and then once they're alone they turn up the volume and start singing along to their favourite song.

That's the proper glum beginning. It would do Gogol proud.

To my annoyance, my story is a common one (we're on to Goncharov now?) – at least, in the important ways. After all, many people are objects by choice (which I certainly am) and PTSD is the *sufferance du jour*, In fact, I had long ago made the decision, at about the age of sixteen, as one did at my bravura-conscious Beverly Hills High School (objectification, not PTSD). My monthly download of the British fashion magazine *Sense and Sensibility* offered continuous confirmation. I'd buy scarfs, shirts, shoes, belts, Euro-spiffy topcoats straight out of the chute and preen (or soil them in the wardrobe, depending).

I connected with the male models. Perfection personified. I wanted to be them or more often I wanted them to take me along, either hand-in-hand or thrown over their shoulder, to wherever they so fixedly strode. My *Carte Bleue* always spiked in the days after a download and perusal. Victoria Carlyle's Editor's Letter amused me, much like the soundtrack to *The*

Rocky Horror Picture Show (and Hell's bells but Bostwick was a hunk back in the day). Ms. Carlyle's pugilistic ribbing of the poorly dressed, be they humble or Royal, often gave me the giggles. I frequently quoted some of her tangier lines, such as her whiplash indictment of an ennobled equestrienne as, "Less well accoutred than the patinaed saddle on which she planted her shall-we-say gruesome derriere." However, in the shadow of my thirtieth birthday, I had begun to feel a worrisome reckoning with objectification. So far, so good. But after thirty? Would I look ridiculous in the silky-svelte outfits in which the muscled twenty-somethings sashayed across sandy beaches?

If it's true that you can judge someone by what he says about others, then I'm dangerously toxic. On the other hand, if you are what you eat, then I'm practically perfect in every way. Go figure. The latter always gives me the titters. When first working in education, we had a Director of Studies who personified the expression 'battle axe.' She had a checklist on an old-fashioned clipboard and waltzed around the school in unchic pant-suit ensembles or knee-length skirts giving orders in the style of Italian fascists or the guards at Sing-Sing. Once, when she flung open the door to the office I shared with a witty English teacher, and she barked something obnoxious at us before flouncing off, my teacher friend turned and said with a deadpan expression, "*Well,* if we are what we eat – *I shudder to think.*" To this day, I can't recall that moment without snickering.

I hesitated at the Saint Michel gate, where Paris' Luxembourg Garden exited to the Place Edmond Rostand. This, of course, is how my story begins; it must, Alpine singing nun allusions aside. As Bette Davis said, and I'm paraphrasing because I've never seen the film (have you?), fasten your seatbelts, it's going to be a bumpy ride – *or flight?* Was that Bette Davis? Anyway, closing my eyes, I configured my protective angels, as suggested to me by my best friend's sister Marigold. Silly, really, since I had believed in neither Heaven nor Hell long before Donald Trump's hog wallow of a Presidency proved once-and-for-all the banality of evil (and the puff-puffery of the American Imperial era). For one thing, I could never devise a fair dividing line. No doubt that's why the Roman Church came up with the ambiguity of Purgatory, though Purgatory would by now be a take-a-number-standing-room-only loony bin, with fat fools in caps throwing rolls of paper towels to starving new arrivals – a place resembling Trump Tower, but mercifully free of gaudy toilet fixtures.

I found my angels beneficial nonetheless; I felt reassured, marching around Paris with a whimsical troop of spirits. It wasn't just any whimsical troop, but a select band of benev-olent cross-dressing Victorian prostitutes, hirsute slaves from ancient Greece, innocents burned at the stake, Roman gladia-tors, unshaved cowboys, medieval nuns. Marigold told me that innumerable angels hung around (those weren't her words, but the gist of the thing) awaiting calls for assistance, so I thought I may as well call on the ones I wanted. Sometimes I wondered if the rich and famous were available. I had tried rousing Gloria Swanson and Oscar Wilde, and once or twice Josephine Baker, but I had no way of knowing if I'd been successful, or even if they had made it to Angelhood.

Post-Traumatic Stress, for which I had been treated for over a year and a half, made my life in Paris a cinematic loop of annoying lucidity, punctuated by panic attacks – not at all like the opening credits of *The Sound of Music*. Two years before, on my mother's only visit to France, a roof-slate fell from my in-laws' château and cleaved her head off, revealing a luxurious wig (*who knew?*). The wig's quality ensured that it survived the slate, like a bloodied ferret (except for the label on what would be its ferret belly). She died in front of me; you don't even bother with CPR or tourniquets on someone decapitated. Afterward, it proved more difficult to get her out of the local village than into it. In fact, the entire village ended up involved, with *Monsieur le Maire* helping to decipher the forms, which demanded a *notaire* to take inventory of three suitcases and a large tote bag purse – and, of course, her wig. The Gendarmes stashed her headless corpse in an emptied and sanitized meat locker at the Carrefour hypermarket in Fontenay-le-Comte since the village had no facilities for a long-term headless-corpse layover.

She might have spent eternity in that supermarket deep freeze, had an efficient woman not appeared from the Consulate in Bordeaux, and with ruthless vigour sorted things out within hours. Thanks to her, my mother and her wigless head were trucked from the meat locker, where they had been concealed in shrouds of cling-wrap, burned to ash, bone bits crushed, remains boxed, wrapped and shipped off to the States before we even had time to mention the wig – which Théophile and I had put through the wash and left to dry on the rarely-used toaster. Being a Vegan, Consulate woman refused our offer for dinner – which happened to be shoulder of lamb – gave us requisite double-cheek kisses and sped off.

Since my mother's death, the Bataclan attacks, the explosions on the St. Petersburg subway and London Tube, the Istanbul and Manchester bombings, the slashings in London, Paris, Marseille and Turku, Finland, the vehicle slaughters in Santa Barbara, Toronto, London, New York, Nice, Berlin, Melbourne, Stockholm, Charlottesville, Barcelona, the shootings in Las Vegas, Parkland, Florida, Santa Fe, Texas and multiple acid attacks from London to Marseilles to Kuala Lumpur, I felt nauseous in crowds, packed in like a pig in an abattoir awaiting slaughter. Concrete bollards offered scant reassurance; the familiar had become fearful. Even the Champs-Elysees had become a shooting range, where a policeman died sitting in his van, at the hands of a kook, who stopped selling drugs long enough to pledge allegiance to a video-game-version of religion. I wanted to live past the worrisome turn-in-the-road of my thirtieth birthday; I preferred wrinkles to bullets, bolts, nails or paralyzed disfigurement. By the way, if you want to increase your odds of suffering from PTSD, read about what bullets from assault rifles do to the human body. They can't be for hunting, those guns. I mean, do hunters want a dead deer with a gargantuan exit wound and pulverized bones everywhere? Could you even eat that meat?

I lost two of my closest friends in the Bataclan massacre, and – face it – to have anyone die in front of you would be shocking; to see your own mother decapitated – that signified. I hadn't liked my mother, but her beheading traumatized me all the same. I had been more upset by the ghastly circumstances than her death itself: spurting blood, the wig on my shoe, her head rolling across the lawn like a hedgehog from *Alice in Wonderland*. Now, after my diagnosis of C-PTSD, and my frantic, fretful, forever-full worrying about my dead friends Didier and Benoît and their bullet-evisceration by an assault rifle whilst at a concert, I thought too often about the roof slate, my mother's open-mouthed head on the ground, the ridiculous wig, and the bizarre aftermath. My friends had been loving, my mother unloving; unlike Didier and Benoît, her death could have been a story you told over beers. Tragic, sure, but comically grotesque. PTSD left no room for humour, apparently.

I looked up the street toward the Pantheon. Despite my urban air of anxiety and my need for shielding angels, the evening had gone well – *so far*. I made the change at Châtelet in seven minutes. Usually, it took ten. Sometimes it took fifteen. Misadventures – high-heeled tourists falling on wet floors, porters on strike, truncheon-wielding police chasing African migrants, pigeons devouring discarded industrial sandwiches – frequently complicated my transfer. And now, I had exited from the park to the busy intersection, where I nervously eyed-up every truck that passed. That, too, had become natural in Paris. Occasionally, everyone balked at a crosswalk, afraid to walk in front of a delivery truck, like frightened Wildebeests at a watering hole. Women with babies in strollers seemed particularly terrified – and rightly so, I always thought. Baby Wildebeests were amongst the first to go, weren't they?

Up the street, the recently steam-cleaned Pantheon glittered with Disney-esque perfection; I had liked it better as a sooty relic, keeping up appearances with ladders in her pantyhose. Feigning an adjustment to my over-the-shoulder satchel, I dallied where three jackbooted CRS police stationed themselves during rush hour. *Compagnies Républicaines de Sécurité*, they were the real thing: broad-shouldered, tall, unshaved. Before the State of Emergency, most Parisians looked kindlier on death and tourists than the CRS, who lurked in wolf packs around corners in dented blue vans. Now, a nightly television story might report an act of brutality in the suburbs and then – radio silence; no official recrimination; nothing. However, they had never intimidated me. On the assumption that with excess testosterone they must play on both teams, I frequently struck provocative poses for them. Today I offered their libido a thin, blond Anglo-Saxon in a tight dress shirt, strap adjusting his satchel.

I saw the incoming phone flash and my best friend Hamish's face appear on the screen beneath the name Ham. He was only ever Ham to his family and me because he loved his name and generally insisted on the full mouth-watering sound of 'Hamish.'

"Is there a bitter but witty gay boy on my phone?" I said.

"My wit is under appreciated and I'm not sure I'm the bitter one in this relationship. But speaking of boys, how were they today?"

"Are. I'm still *chez eux* – and they're suitably erect." I gave the police my best white-toothed winsome smile; I had paid Doctor Korngold (whom I chose because his online photo attracted me) heaps of money for that smile, one of my many efforts to ameliorate turning thirty. The boys smiled back, in their fashion; they really did seem to have permanent erections. A purposeful design in their uniforms? Like plumage on birds to intimidate fledglings? "And the angels are fine as well," I said. "I've collected a nun who was raped by a priest and died in child birth."

"Why can't you –? I mean? *Really*."

"They're all angels, Ham, and Marigold said they're on standby to protect and defend me."

"I can't tell if you're being sarcastic or – what? But you've turned into this, this morbid – thing."

Hamish had been my best friend for twelve years, since we met during Freshman orientation at Princeton. Princeton had been a legacy institution for Hamish, who went straight from the hallowed halls of his exclusive prep school to the equally hallowed halls of Princeton; for Californian me Princeton had been an intellectual, existential leap. I went from my marijuana-perfumed Beverly Hills work-if-you-want-to stylishly laid-back public school to the superficially straitlaced, superciliously scholarly surroundings of Princeton. Now we both lived in Paris, a circumstantial reinforcement of our friendship – a bargain-sealing geographic proximity.

"*Thing*, says my friend the English teacher. Ever so precise. And PTSD tends to do that. It turns one into a morbid – *thing*."

"Whatever. Do they have names, these angels?"

"Possibly Oscar and Gloria. Maybe Josephine."

"But they don't tell you?"

"We don't talk, I don't imagine most of us even speak the same language. We just kind of – commune. Heaven must have a frightful need for translators. Or maybe it's like *Star Trek* and they all just magically communicate."

"I forgot to ask what you wore today," Hamish said. "I know you had a presentation for the big visiting teachers from Berlin."

"Stuttgart, and they weren't big at all – which is the only excuse for being German, so what's that about?" I had started walking again, but paused on the corner to admire myself in a storefront window, "My hot blue shirt and those new shoes I bought at *BHV Homme*, and Théophile's yellow tie – the skinny one I wore on that picnic thing last month? I look like a sexy version of the Swedish flag. Okay, hello," I said to – or at – a sales clerk, who stared out at me from inside the store. "She thinks I'm admiring her over-priced purses. *Oh*. Speaking of which. I have my new satchel."

"The leather one with the cool buckles?"

"*Mais oui*. Meticulously selected by Victoria Carlyle's minions. I'm straight from *Sense and Sensibility's* last edition, page sixty-four, if I remember correctly."

"Oh, good God, you and that magazine. It's pure rubbish," Hamish said.

"It certainly is not. And *pure rubbish* – as opposed to impure rubbish? – sounds like a frightful melange. Take not the name of my Queen in vain. I worship Miss Carlyle." The High Holy Priestess of *Sense and Sensibility*. My idol. One of the world's most beautiful – and wealthy – women, hovering in the after-vicinity of fifty. What she hadn't inherited she made from her magazine empire, whose style magazine *Sense and Sensibility* raked in millions. It had been among the first to go digital and the hard copy still remained the display rag of choice from Chelsea townhouses to fancier dentist offices in fancier suburbs in the Home Counties. Victoria's family had a much-vaunted connection to the last Empress of Austria-Hungary, Amanda Maria delle Grazie Adelgonda Micaela Raffaela Gabriella Giuseppina Antonia Luisa Agnese of Bourbon Parma, who had been, as she termed it in an interview I read, "Ignominiously tossed off the Imperial throne," which she attained late in 1916 – along with her Emperor husband less than two years later.

"Of course," as Victoria put it in another interview, when in a sassy humour, "They were on the throne long enough to get blamed for everything, including trying to negotiate peace, *God forbid* – which apparently irked the Kaiser, who put a stop to it. However, they outlasted those damned Romanovs, who were always messing around in Moldavia. I know – my cousin had a most beautiful estate there."

"Ugh. What's with you, anyway? Are you high?"

"Yes," I said. "We had champagne in the faculty lounge." I held an administrative position in a French Lycée, which meant either all work and no play or all play and no work, depending on the direction of the wind or the vicissitudes of our Proviseur and *Le ministère de l'éducation.* "Today is Félicité-Hélène's – God, I don't know – anniversary or something. Whatever it was, it was worth a couple of bottles of Veuve."

"Where are you now?"

"Just waiting to cross what's it –?" I said. "You?"

"Running down the hill to the station. Can't you hear me wheezing?"

"I hoped you were having a quickie in the janitor's closet."

"What janitor's closet?"

"It's a concept," I told him, "not an actual location."

"Would I be talking on the phone?"

"It's a Hell of a lot easier than texting, and I called you once from – where? A train station in Amsterdam?"

"Copenhagen waiting room, a men's toilet stall, at two in the morning."

"That's right," I said. "So clean that Danish toilet stall, not at all what you expect from a men's room. And you can have an enjoyable time in a janitor's closet. You just have to find a man with a strong back. Remember that Australian guy Kyle? We tried it standing up – which is the janitor closet idea – in Luxembourg Garden, but we ended upside down behind that stupid marionette shack. Kyle did not have a strong back. *Va te faire foutre,*" I yelled at a car that roared past with a toot of its horn. "Later, Ham."

"Later, Justin."

I stood nude in front of the bathroom mirror in a Renoir-esque pose. The tiled bathroom – a refit with faux marble counters and top of the line double-flush toilet – sparkled. Our *femme de ménage* had been today, her handiwork visibly aromatic. Through the open bathroom door, above the windows, I saw the mansard roof of a neighbouring building. My change of clothes – shirt, jeans, light cotton sweater – rested on the chair. In the winter, I draped them over the radiator so that they were toasty when I put them on. Handy that way, radiators. I followed my evening ritual: A quick shopping run through the Marks & Spencer food hall on Rue Mabillon, home to unload, a shower, a change of clothes, and then off for a drink with my friends. My husband Théophile usually arrived from his fashionable office in La Défense while I sipped high-octane beverages with the gang. Dinner came sometime after that, depending on Théophile's or my mood.

I continued to stare at my hairless – most of it natural, some of it cosmetic, as one does – nude splendour, then turning to look at the clock, saw that I needed to hurry, grabbed my clothes and went down the hall to the bedroom. As usual, I fretted a moment about leaving a note – sometimes I did, mostly I didn't. Théophile knew where I was, and he never seemed to care. A pro forma exercise, like so much else in my life, the notes always lay where I left them; I couldn't tell if Théophile read them. Stealthy in a wealthy Avenue Foch way, the only child of an esteemed family that had survived revolution, evolution, war, international financial collapse and Socialist predation, Théophile stood to inherit lots of Leg-rêle-Chevrier money and property. We'd been married now for six years, had this huge apartment (though, strictly speaking, it still belonged to Théophile's parents), a villa in the mountains above Evian (you'd call it a condominium in the States) and the use of a country house in the Vendée, where my mother had lost her head.

A handsome French husband, skilful in bed, well-heeled and – in point of fact, these days Théophile seemed not merely less skilled in bed, but uninterested and critical of odd things, like whether I had shaved in the areas where he liked me to shave.

I snapped at him the other night, "Turn on the light and look for yourself, goddamn it."

A recent quirk, screwing in the dark.

"I should have married Campbell when he asked me," I said.
"He *never*." Hamish said in undisguised surprise.

"Twice. That I can remember, at any rate. Once he suggested running off to Québec and honeymooning in the Chateau Frontenac."

"When?"

"One summer."

Our gaggle of friends, Hamish, Javier, Nicolas and me, had been sitting far too long in our corner table, surrounded by music and a linguistic smorgasbord; English speakers tried ordering in French, everyone else from Swedes to Argentines tried ordering in accented English. A bar from *Star Wars*. Yet none of us made a move to leave.

"I wish you would not talk about important matters in this fashion," Nicolas told me, though not unkindly; he had a deep voice and one of those high-end cultured accents. "It isn't," he searched his English vocabulary. "Seemly."

Classically handsome Nicolas – with his ubiquitously sophisticated French face – worked for a publishing house, possibly as an editor. He had enough money to live well, so editor got more votes than drudge. Then again, he could be one of those pampered French sons – the beneficiary of mom and dad's largesse, while his impoverished sister ate take-away dinners after her dull work in Nantes or Angers, a Balzac novel in modern dress.

"*Seemly*? What dictionary did you pull that out of, Mildred?"

"The dictionary of my clogged mind," he said, winking and standing up.

I liked the way he pronounced the word as clog-*ED*.

"Now. It is time for me to be leaving," he said.

The moment had been inevitable, of course, the end of the evening. I shifted slightly and light fell on my face. Someone at the bar turned to look at me – as always.

"Do you have a sister in Nantes or Angers?" I asked.

Nicolas looked perplexed. He sat back down. "I have one sister and she lives with me in Paris. Why do you connect her to those places?"

"I was thinking about Balzac, you know, like *Les illusions perdues* and Lucien de Rubempré and his sisters back in the provinces who – "

"Lucien Chardon," Nicolas corrected me, in that sincere way of his, which I occasionally mocked. "He only tries to change his name to de Rubempré because he finds maybe an aristocratic connection in his mother's family – you know, for some social advancement. It is not unlike *Tess of the d'Urbervilles*, by Thomas 'Ardy." Despite the virtual perfection of his English, Nicolas had still failed to master the ever-challenging Anglo-Saxon 'H'.

"Just shoot me," Hamish said.

I nearly made my hand into a gun to pretend to shoot him with my thumb and index finger, as I would have done in the before time, but instead I twitched nervously and looked at Nicolas as if for – what? Comfort? *Help*?

"Come to think of it," Hamish said. "I didn't know you had a sister." "Generally, people do not wish to hear about your sister," Nicolas said

"Though mine is extraordinary. She is intelligent, kind and successful."

"What kind of world is it where those traits count as extraordinary?" I said. "But I suppose people are more inclined to hear sister stories when they involve Welsh surfers and multiple children." I looked at Javier and Nicolas; their blank stares made clear that they hadn't read any of the stories online or in the tabloids; peculiar as that was, I rather admired them for it. "Marigold – that's Hamish's sister – was living in Cape Town with a white policeman named Nethersole. I kid you not.

Nethersole. Such a freakishly butch name. But then Marigold's always been arty about male beauty – forever dating these to-die-for gorgeous guys with tattoos and missing fingers and fused earlobes."

"*Fused earlobes?*" Hamish said.

"It's true. We called him earlobe guy. He was from Tennessee or one of those other places the studly guys drain out of." I knew that Hamish's first love had been a man from Tennessee, so I often used it in stories. It had been my mother's way; it had been my grandmother's; a streak of wickedness encoded in my DNA? "Nethersole she met at a disco in Switzerland. I forget where. Well, Geneva or Zurich, obviously." I shrugged at the irrelevance of the locale. "Anyway, once she was in Cape Town, getting Nethersole's nightly once-over, she discovered surfing. Apparently, she was good at it – surfing, I mean, but presumably fucking Nethersole too. Though how one judges competence in surfing, I've no idea. Competence in fucking I understand."

"Radical controlled manoeuvres," Javier said.

I looked at Javier who in turn – while sipping his beer – stared at Hamish with an indecipherable expression. A botanist for the *Jardin des plantes*, sexy Javier had appeared in our group about a year ago and had been dating Hamish for the last five months. He regularly appeared on breakfast television talking about plants. With the build of a weekend athlete – muscled, broad chested, long legged, his good looks and television appearances had earned him our group label telegenic, as in, 'Where is your telegenic boyfriend, Hamish?' As I remember saying, "They don't put a hunk o' man like that on Télématin just because he knows ten different types of geraniums."

After a last lingering glance at Hamish, Javier continued, "*On l'indique ainsi en anglais*: manoeuvres close to the curl, wave selection, longest functional distance – that's it, basically."

"You surf?" Hamish asked.

"Yes."

"I didn't know Spain was a big surfing spot," I said.

"To my knowledge, it is not. I have never surfed in Spain. When in Spain, I only visit with my family – and eat."

Another musically punctuated silence.

"Wise man. Choose food over sport whenever possible. Anyway," I continued. "It was in a surfing competition that Marigold met Gareth, who's a Welsh immigrant to Australia – though, obviously, he was in South Africa surfing. And that is how, having dumped Nethersole, Marigold ended up down under, married with five kids in seven years." I made a moue of disgust.

"He's a nice guy, Gareth," Hamish said, as if my story had indicated otherwise – which it did not. I had been thinking of Marigold's stretch marks. "I like him."

"Potent, clearly. He must be a big seller in Aussie sperm banks. He probably exports the stuff. There's supposed to be a dearth of quality sperm. Everybody's been decimated by antibiotics, pesticides and oestrogen. Except for Gareth. Gareth obviously hasn't been decimated. There could be little Gareths from Hong Kong to Stockholm – more recognizable in Stockholm, I presume."

"Oestrogen?" Hamish wondered.

"It's in things you eat – or breathe. I don't know where it comes from. Google, it, you'll see I'm right."

"He has an arty beauty, the potent Gareth?" Nicolas asked.

"He's totally sexy," Hamish said. "Blond, thin nose – beautiful black chest hair."

I gave a there-we-are gesture. "See? That's an arty combination – blond head hair and black chest hair."

"I assume your sister doesn't surf?" I asked Nicolas.

"Not unless she has taken it up since this morning. She is a *Juges d'instruction* and busy, and Paris is far from the ocean, so I doubt it. Unfortunately, my chest hair matches the hair on my head, so I think I do not have an arty beauty. My sister calls herself Hortense Louise and she has not so intriguing a story as your sister, Hamish."

"Few do, although mine's been known to cut her hair off as an act of protest and now raises goats."

"Marigold spent time on a commune, and I think they raised goats there too."

Since the word commune had a completely different meaning in French, where it indicated all the geographic areas of a city or town, Nicolas looked momentarily baffled.

"That wasn't a commune," I said, "get real. It was an expensive piece of rolling wooded real estate in upstate New York, financed by your parents and Marigold's then hunky boyfriend's drug money. My sister should be so wise as to sell drugs. But *Hortense?*" I said. "What did your parents – like, were they dropping acid or something? Where in the purple Hell did they find that name? Hortense?"

"We have family names." Nicolas had been shuffling through the photos on his phone and finally tapped one of a brunette in judicial robe and cravat. "This is she. I do not believe my parents ever experimented with drugs. But if they did, it had nothing to do with our names. Our names are historical. I have a great uncle calling himself Nicolas and our grandmother calls herself Hortense."

"What was that you said about Balzac?" I asked Hamish. "You're on to something."

"This sounds more Proust than Balzac."

Nicolas shrugged. "I don't see why my sister's name is any more peculiar than calling yourself the name of Justin, which means 'healer.' It is possibly the Anglicized version of the Spanish name for the flower you call hyacinth."

Everyone stared at him; a typical Nicolas moment.

"I rather like the idea of wearing hyacinth," I said, although I had no idea what hyacinth even looked like or if it even smelled nice. "And as a school administrator in France, where no one heeds a word I say or write, it sounds ironic, which is the truest definition of my job."

Nicolas's eyes glittered thoughtfully a moment, then he said, "I like being the brave protector, which is the meaning of Nicolas."

"Do you?" I said. "A boy does like being bravely protected from time to time." Then, "Ham's parents *were* doing drugs, by the way."

"Quite true," Hamish agreed. "However, they're also family names. My mother was in an ancestral nostalgia phase when my brother and I were born. Hamish and Campbell. My great uncles."

"Poor old things," I said.

Nicolas put his phone back in his suit pocket.

Javier had just taken Hamish's hand in his own, which caught my eye. "Ignoring the surfing thing, you're telegenically quiet tonight."

"Silence is effective communication."

"Like – *what?* It promotes enjoyable conversation?" I stared at him. "That was me responding silently. However, since you haven't thrown your beer in my face, I'm clearly not fluent." He finished his drink. "Don't worry, I get it. You're the virile Hamish archetype. This archetype is something Ham and I share. We like 'em manly, strong, hairy and – well, I was going to say silent, but honestly the silent part is not as crucial as a hairy chest and bedroom dominance – a boy's been known to make many accommodations in the chatterbox area. Maslow's archetypes of love. It's all by the script, isn't it?"

"Yes. Maslow's archetypes of love are true," Nicolas said. "I am *actif* and only *actif*, thus I always am looking for a man who will let me – "

"Oh, for fuck's sake," I said. "And pun intended. Did I ask to look at everyone's dance card?" I searched for my satchel under my chair. "I'm going to get this thing stolen again, I swear." I gestured toward a waif-thin migrant of some un-known Middle Eastern or North African origin, standing by the stairwell, a gold chain hanging on his neck like a price tag. After a moment, I said, "Think he's a hooker?"

"The other choice would be –?" Hamish asked.

I watched the young man a moment or two, reflecting on the fact that Nicolas said he was '*actif*.' I wondered why Hamish hadn't yet developed one of his famously intense crushes on Nicolas, who *did* have an arty and masculine beauty, with his bright blue eyes, perpetual five o'clock shadow, and a hairy chest from which unruly hairs occasionally peeped over the top of unbuttoned shirts. My friends generally shared my *passif* inclinations – or 'my tendencies' as my mother had termed them – and thus we shopped, beached ourselves at Deauville, and hunted men (or pretended to hunt), in a pack. Nicolas, whom Didier, Benoît and I met together at a party, represented the exception that proved the rule. I liked Nicolas. Of all my friends, Nicolas alone seemed both soft and strong; a really remarkable combination.

Hamish looked at me. "I feel sorry for those guys. No pa-pers, no work, no hope."

"There's always the hope of snagging my satchel," I said, tucking it in my lap.

"And you should have married Campbell. He's hung like a horse."

"Perhaps that's why I remember his proposals, then. And who says Campbell is hung like a horse? Campbell? He's always been prone to exaggeration." I looked then at Javier, who held my gaze until he turned away with a blush. Everyone laughed, but cautiously now, edgy. I knew how to make people edgy; I did it recklessly, I had since Middle School, sometimes disliking myself for it afterward – sometimes feeling a sense of accomplishment. Sadly, this skill came to me naturally, also through my mother and grandmother, women I loathed – unlike Hamish's mother, whom I occasionally saw as an adopted mother figure.

We finished getting our things together and then pushed our way through to the door and out to the corner. In a ritualistic pattern, we said our good nights, around the circle, air kisses on each cheek, Justin and Hamish always saying goodbye twice and holding hands.

"Are you really *actif?*" I asked Nicolas, whose heavy satchel, thrown across his shoulder made his chest seem even bigger, and it seemed suddenly evident that he would be only *actif.*

"Of course. Everyone knows this."

"Everyone, apparently, did not know this," I said. "Perhaps Didier knew it, but Benoît and I – and everyone else," and I pointed at Hamish, "Were not in the know. Now. We're on for my upcoming birthday *fête?*"

"Sure," Hamish said. "But mixing social groups? It's bad luck or something. Very scary mojo."

"What mixing social groups? There's no mixing, don't be weird. And 'very scary,' says Bulwer-Lytton." I shrugged. "No worries, I'll put out fresh garlic and chicken blood. It'll be fine."

"It won't. Every time I'm over there I feel this glacier moving through your apartment."

"*Glacier?* Why have you become so odd about coming over to our apartment? You used to live in my *salon*, watching television and drinking up Théophile's wine collection."

"It's just – I don't know, Théophile makes me uncomfortable sometimes."

"Huh. Butch piece of work that he is. He didn't used to bother you. Are you secretly in love with him?"

"I am not, I assure you."

"Then promise to come to my party with a bouquet of flowers, preferably freesias. It's my birthday. I'm turning thirty, the crypt door is opening wide in welcome. I want everyone there. Please?"

"Did Campbell really ask you to marry him?"

"It bothers you?" I asked

"A little," Hamish said, "if it's true."

We looked too long at one another, a caustically binding gaze. "You knew we were at it like gibbons. He fucked my lights out for two entire summers. We woke up entire neighbourhoods."

"You said one summer."

"Then I lied. How unlike me."

We regarded one another – hyenas at a watering hole – on the verge of baring our teeth.

Hamish blinked first. "You had a pulse and were available, though those weren't always requirements back in the day. Campbell fucked light sockets and inner tubes, as I recall."

Again, we looked at each other; this time we both blinked.

"You are, as always, forgiven for your nastiness," I said. "I know you are broken and twisted and cannot help thyself."

Hamish smiled back. Then we broke apart and I headed home.

The buzzer awoke me from a deep sleep. However, looking at the bedside clock I realized I'd only been in bed an hour and the emptiness beside me meant that Théophile had yet to come home. When the buzzer sounded again, I leapt from the covers and went down the hall to the intercom. "*Qui est là?*"

"Justin?"

"*India?*"

"And Campbell too. Buzz us up, sweetie. We'll attract the paparazzi out here." In the background, I heard Campbell saying, 'You wish.'

"Buzz, buzz, buzz?" India said.

I pressed the lever and a door clicked far away. Returning to the bedroom, I found a shirt and jeans. Just buttoning up when they knocked, there they were, Hamish's mother and brother: India Chatterton, beautiful as ever, in a crisp haircut that turned her grey hair into a designer accessory, and Campbell – tall and striking, maybe a bit thinner, with a trendy beard around his face.

"*Justin,*" India cried, pulling me into a tight hug. Despite decades in the United States, an American husband and thoroughly American children – albeit with a penchant for living abroad – India still sounded like the upper crust suburban girl from High Wycombe she had once been. It was her core identity, summed up in interviews as, "Buckinghamshire born and bred." It would be her epitaph.

Disengaging myself from India's grip, I brought them inside – where we stood in the living room looking at one another. "Was I meant to be expecting you?" I asked.

"I have no idea," India said, snooping through the windows at one of the elegant apartments across the courtyard. "Such delightful décor over there, original and modish. I should snap some photos for Nate Berkus."

"Hey, Justin," Campbell said, taking me into a half embrace and clapping me on the back.

"Hi, Campbell. Have you lost weight?"

"Been working out," Campbell said, pulling his T-shirt up over his head. "Check out the six pack and pecs."

"He's doing modelling now," India said, waving a hand at her son's bare chest. "You know how our Campbell throws himself into these projects."

"Nude modelling?" I asked.

"Maybe," Campbell said. "Shirtless, sure. I don't think porn or anything." He rippled his chest muscles at me, laughed, and put his shirt back on. "I'm thinking maybe movies after. You know how modelling gets you noticed."

"I certainly notice the models in *Sense and Sensibility*," I said, "Victoria Carlyle chooses some lookers."

"*Pooh*," India said, "That démodé rag."

"It is anything but, and you sound like Hamish. That magazine is my guide to life. Sit, sit," I said. "I'll make some tea or something. Théophile's still at work, it seems, so he may come charging in exhausted at any moment. Do you want tea?"

"Tisane," India said. "Something without caffeine? You have tisane?"

"I don't know." I put my hands on the top of my head, confused and sleepy. "Chamomile. I have some Chamomile. Is that all right?"

"No. Mint. Don't you have mint, darling?"

I turned around and stepped into the kitchen, hoping to Hell that the maid had left some of her flavoured teas behind. She had. Success. "What do you know? I do. Campbell?"

"Water. You must have water."

"Yes, I must have." I put a beaker of tap water and a teabag into the microwave and poured Campbell a glass of Wattwiller mineral water. I took Campbell's glass out to him while waiting for the water and tea bag to boil. Théophile would disapprove if he saw me boiling the teabag with the water, but I always did it anyway; it saved time. "Here," I said, handing the water to Campbell. "Now. What the Hell –?"

"What the Hell what?" India wondered, tossing her lovely wedge of hair.

"What the Hell are you two doing unannounced in my apartment in the middle of the night?"

"Sounds like the opening line of Polish porn," India said. "It's all the rage now, Polish porn. I wonder if they'll make you learn Polish," she said to Campbell.

"I'm not doing porn and you don't have opening lines, mom, you only have to know five things – right, like 'more, more' and 'give it to me, baby.' I could probably say all that in Polish if I had to."

"You were married to an Italian and never even learned to count to ten."

"I did – actually, to twenty, I believe."

India gestured toward the clock on a bookcase. "It most certainly is not the middle of the night – and we're visiting you, Justin. We've just arrived. *Nous venons d'arriver.* We took that morning flight from JFK that Balfour loves so much. Personally, it seems like a complete waste of your day. By the time we got over to the 8th, where Balfour insists on staying – though it's beyond even borderline fashionable, I mean it did have that resurgence a couple of years ago it's true, but now it's all wealthy Moroccans and nouveaux riches Eastern Europeans – pooh, the day was over. Anyway, we unpacked, showered, reconnoitred and – *voilà*. Here we are." She pointed an orange-red fingernail toward the kitchen. "My tea, darling? I can hear it boiling away in there, bag, cup, sugar, spoon and all."

"Sorry." I returned to the kitchen, pulled out the tea bag, plopped it into the trash, poured the greenish-water into a mug, took a deep breath and then carried the tea out to India.

"It's looking good," Campbell said, motioning around at the apartment.

"Pretty much the same as the last time you were here. We did have that wall painted."

"Cool. That's such a great fireplace thing."

"Thanks. And it's a fireplace."

Campbell looked confused, but I left him mired in it.

"You're a Nate Berkus groupie too, I can tell," India said, wiggling a finger at some lined wicker baskets. "I sat next to him at a dinner last month at the Met. He'd be perfect for Hamish. Jewish boy with good values, lovely hair, winning smile and such panache – and that unshaved look you and my son prefer."

"Who the heck are we talking about?" Campbell asked.

"A Chicago and New York designer," I told him.

"And much more," India said. "He's got a cult following: television, photos on refrigerators, autographed scarves, centre-fold spreads. It looks like a stage set, your apartment. Like something from an operetta. You live on a stage set."

Why be so unkind, I thought. Had I irritated her? Clearly best to roll with the punch. "Like – what? *La fille du régiment?*"

"I was thinking more Offenbach," India opened her hand in the direction of the velvet drapes. "Perhaps *Orphée aux Enfers?*"

I could have mentioned that the drapes had been there when we moved in, no doubt chosen by Théophile's Gorgon of a mother, but it felt futile – I felt, somehow, as if India's grousing had nothing at all to do with me or the apartment. "Campbell, do you remember asking me to marry you?"

Campbell gulped some water. "Maybe. We had some wild summers in our time."

"Surely you remember asking me to marry you."

"Campbell?" India scoffed. "That's precisely the thing I would *not* expect him to remember. Fortunately, he does recall that he is finally – finally – divorced from *Foro bagnato gigante*."

"For the hundredth time, that's not his name, mom," Campbell said, shaking his head. "He's Giuseppe Marco Salvatore."

India sipped her tea. "And here I've been calling him that for years."

Being back among Hamish's family meant hearing India refer to her son's ex-husband as the 'giant wet hole,' which I suspected Campbell knew full well.

"His lawyers' vicious divorce hagglings at least demonstrated *why* he married our Campbell, besides the fact that he's porn-worthy, of course. Because we're rich. That's why. Balfour's family is more American than apple pie – in fact, they pre-date apple pies. They've been around looting and amassing fortunes since the mid-1600s, and that ancestral tree of his has everything in it from gibbons to senators to murderous crooks to captains of commerce – and occasionally all in one lifetime." She smiled, her way of making peace. "It's one of America's finest families." She patted Campbell's hand.

"So, dear, we're here for two weeks," India said to me, "more if we take the place in La Rochelle."

"What place in La Rochelle?" I asked.

"Helena Sinclair's."

"Who the Hell is Helena Sinclair?"

"Her daughter married a Frenchman," India said.

"I know we went at it like heathens," Campbell said without looking at me, his cheeks flushed above his beard. "We were for sure a pair of crazy monkeys."

"So, you do remember asking?"

"Maybe – you know – one of those throes of passion things."

I stood up, from where I'd been leaning against the wide lower shelf of a bookcase and went to stand at the *portes-fenêtres*.

The shadowy courtyard felt mysterious, with glimmers of light from various rooms on various floors. I thought I saw one of the building's cats walking along a rain gutter across the way. When I turned back toward the living room, I met India's eyes – and we seemed to communicate with one another, though I could not have said what.

"Something's bothering you," I said. "Have you lost weight?"

"Indeed, I have. A few kilos. And something's bothering *you*," she said back at me.

"Besides having PTSD and being dragged out of bed unexpectedly? But you're changing the subject. What's up with you?"

She waved a dismissive hand. "This tea is atrocious. Are you sure it's mint?"

"So it said."

"Now," India said, "Tell us all about Javier."

"Hamish said he hadn't mentioned Javier yet."

"That doesn't answer the question."

I went to the love seat and perched on the arm nearest Campbell. "You've been corresponding with Théophile, haven't you?"

Campbell shrugged his lack of complicity, but India waved a hand. "If one calls email and texting corresponding. Do you call email and texting corresponding? I don't. It's like shouting down the alley to the neighbour in curlers. It's not real correspondence at all."

"I'll take that fanciful imagery as a yes. You're coming to my party, aren't you? That's why you're here, I trust."

"Terrific invitations," Campbell said. "You're so fucking creative. I've kept mine."

"Of course, that's why we're here," India said. "Though Balfour couldn't resist a bit of self-promotion as well. He's giving a reading. We'll all have to make an appearance." She sighed. "And Javier? You've begged that question entirely, pumpkin."

"What has Théophile told you?"

"Oh, good God. Honestly, Justin. This tea is undrinkable." India put it on the floor beside her. "He loves Hamish, but Ham doesn't love him back, since he distrusts love because he fears it will lead to heartache. This is par for the course with children from dysfunctional families."

"I can't imagine my husband saying *any* of that, even under the effects of LSD, which I assure you he has never taken."

"Never say never, Poppet, and I may have interpreted a bit; one must with men, especially Frenchmen. You must know that."

"Théophile never writes to me," Campbell said.

"Javier's a nice guy," I offered. "I like him. You'll see him at the party – though he didn't get one of those grand invites."

"Wonderfully illuminating. *A nice guy*. I'll ponder that." India stood up.

"As I shall ponder a fluttering hand as response to what's bothering you enough to make you lose two dress sizes," I said.

"Ever so dangerously clever, young man. You need to get back to bed, I can see that. I thought people in Paris kept New York hours."

"I wouldn't know. I'm nearly thirty. I'm old. I watch *N'oubliez pas les paroles* and the news and then go to bed."

India pulled me into another hug. "*Old*. Don't be silly. I just called you young. Would I lie? Dinner tomorrow – our treat – bang up affair. Everyone's invited. I'll send you the co-ordinates. Come on, Campbell, bring those off-the-rack Pecs of yours and let's find another taxi. Do they still have that taxi rank by the Hôtel de Ville? Or should we use a service?"

"Yes, and Yes," I said.

"Right then, à *demain*." India kissed my cheeks. "You look good, darling."

"Gorgeous, as always," Campbell said.

2

I stood at the window feeling lonely and observed the neighbours watching a film. My eyes welled with tears and I closed
them against the pain.

I tried not to think about the night Didier and Benoît
died at the Bataclan. However, trying had never yet stopped
my thoughts. Every detail of the evening still felt so fresh, how
I met up with Théophile and my friends for Didier's birthday
– the fact that Théophile hadn't shaved and wore a blue shirt
with a loosely knotted Feraud tie. I'd met Didier and Benoît
when we worked together, years ago; they were my first French
friends. It had been an enjoyable evening. We finished our
dinners, kissed our goodbyes, and then Théophile and I took
a car home and Didier and Benoît went to the concert at the
Bataclan. There had been no penumbra of tragedy, no one
said, "I wonder if we'll die tonight?" We went to dinner at
Didier's favourite restaurant and then Didier and Benoît were
eviscerated as they sat listening to music; long ago cremated
and scattered together in Fontainebleau Forest, where they had
enjoyed hiking, a ceremony excruciatingly fresh in my anguish,
the faces of their mothers, fathers, sisters, brothers on that cold,
foggy day when we scattered the ashes.

When I opened my eyes, someone had been shot in the film the neighbours watched; a woman with erect nipples screamed. During all this time at the window, I had scrutinised a piece of metal, which clung to the bottom corner of the window frame. It called out to me and I answered, pressing my hand against the jagged edge, as blissful as a coital rush. I pressed my hand against spikey metal and bled, dripping blood down into the darkness of the courtyard. Over this, I had control. Nothing made sense in my life, except this drip, drip of blood. Well, it also made sense that my father had found an excuse not to hither hence from Beverly Hills, even for my thirtieth birthday – but that fell into the same category as knowing the sun would rise and the earth would spin. It signified nothing. Understandably, my father would never come to France, the place where his wife – quite literally – lost her mind; why should he?

Almost two-thirty, the courtyard dark now, and Théophile had neither come home nor left a message. I went into the kitchen and lit a cigarette, a habit I'd recently taken up on the sly. I studied a cactus, nestled in a Little Prince ceramic pot. It sat on the window ledge where it got most light; Hamish had put it there. Hamish persisted in buying me Little Prince objects under the illusion that I liked them. I did not. When I was little, my *au pair* – yes, my parents who couldn't cough up the coinage for a private school found the funds for a full-time nanny – had a plant like this, a Christmas cactus she called it. Like octopus tentacles, it stretched toward something, waving its globules of pink blossoms on gnarled stalks. It lacked any beauty, my midnight companion, with changes only I noticed: growth, decay of blossoms, subtle metamorphosis. I wished my father *would* come to Paris for my thirtieth, even though

I detested the thought of him coming to Paris – no doubt as much as he detested the thought of ever coming, whatever the occasion. How could such opposing feelings reconcile?

Almost every night now, I came out to the kitchen, lit up, and stared at the cactus. I hated the image of myself staring at a potted plant, though I only noticed it because I needed something to focus on. It needed dusting. I'd leave a note for the maid. A film of brown muck encrusted the ridges. If I had the energy, I'd find a cloth and clean it myself. Instead, I blew a cloud of grey smoke at it. Did anyone notice me as carefully as I noticed that fucking plant? In a fashion that might reveal my own metamorphosis? When I told Hamish about my PTSD changes since the Bataclan – weight loss, bags under my eyes, purple shadows of exhaustion – he dutifully claimed to fret on my behalf. However, Hamish fretted with the same intensity about the Amazon rain forest. His disquiet didn't say much about me. Théophile? He had suggested the proper pill-popping psychiatrist: that represented his contribution. I felt as if Théophile noticed me now in the same way a ship's captain keeps a lighthouse in her line of sight so as not to run aground. Théophile hadn't noticed when I recently changed my hair – or if he did, he kept silent – and he said nothing these days when I bought new shirts and body-hugging trousers.

If I looked long in the mirror, what did *I* see? A permanent bagginess under my right eye, a deepening crow's foot from the corner of that eye back toward my hairline, a vile black hair that kept re-growing on my left ear? I wasn't in touch with my own metamorphosis either. Sighing, I blew another smoke cloud at the cactus. Sometimes I tried to recall compelling moments of my life – and could not. I recalled little besides that cinematic loop from my mother's beheading to the night of the Bataclan. For instance, I would not be able to remember the name of the last movie I'd seen, or my favourite aunt's name, or the name of the kitten I adopted one summer. What the Hell was that cat's name anyway? It eluded me. If ever I had told him, Théophile would remember. Théophile remembered every fucking thing he heard. What did this forgetfulness mean, I wondered? What did it say about the profundity of my post-Bataclan desperation? The pill-popping psychiatrist gave me helpful medication and said, "What do *you* think it means?"

I had a friend one summer, staying with his grandmother next door. Irish red hair, giggles, great fun this friend. So, what was his name? It had always rolled right off my tongue that name, I'd told stories about our escapades so many times – our shared crush on his grandmother's cinema handsome shirtless gardener. Always this summer friend's name tripped into the breach. Tom? No, T-something, though. Tyler? No. I sighed angrily, stubbed out my cigarette, got up and walked down the hallway to the salon. Hamish affectionately called our apartment – which, curiously, he now avoided – "hallway house," since it had an array of hallways as its defining architectural feature: down the side along the bedrooms, to the bathroom, to the toilet, to the kitchen. We lost more square footage to hallway than most people had for an entire apartment.

I considered calling Hamish, but he would have been asleep for hours, or – quite randomly – my sister in Hawaii, though we hadn't talked in over two years and I wasn't sure that I could either find her number or easily discern the time of day or night on Maui. Instead, I went to the open *porte-fenêtre* that gave on to the large cobbled courtyard. The air at the window felt fresher. My heart raced. As always, I found these sudden wild emotions alarming. I tried deep breathing; I tried counting to fifty. Either one of those often calmed me down before things bloomed into a panic attack. I leaned against a doorframe and watched the activity in the apartment across from the way. A man in his underwear prissily hung out his laundry on an expensive folding rack, close to the window. No one in Paris – or virtually no one – had tumble dryers, even the sort found in Manhattan high rises. The energy companies and the government viewed them as ecologically evil and punished you appropriately.

Although the window grips hurt my thighs, I sat on the ledge and stared into the courtyard. Maybe I should light up another cigarette? It would be more picturesque, sitting there smoking. The horny neighbour on the third floor would be aroused. What did cigarettes do exactly? Did they calm you down? Perhaps they perked you up? People smoked them at breakfast, didn't they? I'd never smoked for any other reason than simply doing it, so I had no idea what purpose they served. If I remembered, I'd ask Hamish. Hamish knew about things like why people smoked. Hamish might even know why I wandered around the apartment like this night after night after fucking night. Pre-birthday jitters? Bataclan trauma? The beginning of the end for anyone beautiful? I lived out the lyrics of a Lana del Rey song. People who have built their success off their looks should be able to collect their pensions at thirty and retire to a chalet in Switzerland.

Then, I stood up, went to the computer, logged on, went into my music folder, and clicked on Arkol's album *Fait Divers*. I loved the angry-urgent plea of *"Qu'est-ce que tu fais toi demain?"* I put on Théophile's Bose headphones. 'What are *you* doing tomorrow?' Arkol demanded.

"Justin?" Théophile asked, startled, as we lay together in early morning light.

41

I buried my face against his furry chest and sobbed. "I don't know what's the matter with me," I blubbered. "I'm so afraid, Théophile, that it will happen to us, somewhere, somehow, and I miss them – but it's not only that I miss them, it's that I think of their final moments, of the terror, the hot bullets, the sense of confusion, the – "

"*Shhh.* Take a bath and half a Xanax," Théophile interrupted me. "It's a work day, and unless you want to phone in ill, you'll need to be tough. You always feel better after a bath."

I lifted my face and gently kissed Théophile's mouth, both of his eyes. He smiled, but thinly, chary of this wounded abundance of sentiment.

"Do you still want me, Théophile?"

"Want you?"

"Do you still – God, I don't know – *desire* me?"

"Of course, I do," he said, but without the force I wanted – that I needed.

"And you love me?"

He stroked my hair, kissed my forehead, and I felt rather than saw his vexed expression, the bewildered drawing together of his brows. "Now," he said, "you take a bath. I am going to read."

"Still reading Mitterrand's biography?"

"Yes. And they are still telling me that he was a crook," he said. "My childhood hero. A bath?" Théophile, with his simmering blue-grey eyes, and such elegant detachment from life's petty concerns.

"Yes," I said, "Okay."

When India and I came through the connecting door to his room, Campbell stood in his boxer shorts at the hotel window, looking down on the Paris street scene, listening to music. He hadn't answered our persistent knocking.

India waved her hand in front of his face.

"*Holy Hell, mom.* Oh, hi, Justin."

"Put some clothes on for God's sake," India said. "Your father's already waiting in the bar. Not that he minds waiting in bars. Why have you suddenly become naked man?"

"What suddenly? This is me. And I'm not naked, I'm wearing underwear."

"Consider me put in my place, then."

"What were you listening to?" I asked him.

"Madonna, 'I love New York,' It has such great lyrics that song, Madonna at her best. Despite that pumpkin-headed make-believe President giving the word a bad name, I love the way our Madge says 'pussy,' right in the middle of the song."

Some perplexed, painful truth passed between us, sizzling like a short circuit.

"Hurry up, already," India said.

Campbell shrugged, as he turned away from me and looked for some clothes. Tugging on a pair of jeans, he said, ""You're so cute in that shirt."

"I know," I said. "That's why I wore it." I twirled. "The outward sign of my inner grace?"

"Wouldn't that mean ugly people have no inner grace?"

"They don't."

"How come you didn't tell Hamish we were coming?" Campbell asked India.

"You know, I'm embarrassed about that." She went to the window Campbell had just vacated. "I thought Justin told him. I'm sure I asked you to."

I shook my head. "You did *not*, India."

"You should have told him yourself, mom," Campbell said, choosing a T-shirt from a pile in his unpacked suitcase. "That's the way one does it."

"Yes. I know."

"*So –?*"

India leaned quietly against the window. After a lengthy inspection of the street she said, "I do many strange things. But, then, it's our way."

"*Our?* Who do you mean by 'our?' Is this one of those Englishie things you pull out when it suits you?"

"Oh, good Lord, Campbell. You do put my back up. No, our as in our family."

"Yeah, okay, I accept that," he said, searching unsuccessfully for a pair of socks.

"Maybe I was punishing him."

"Hamish?" I asked. "Why?"

"Just being mean to him," she said. "Spiteful. I resent him, I think."

"Why would you possibly resent Hamish?" Campbell asked. He at last found a pair of socks and struggled to put them on while leaning against the bed. "He's the nicest of us all."

"Something about how he – you know – escaped, hidden away from the hurly-burly, tucked away in his nicey-nice life here in Paris. It irks me."

"Then doesn't Marigold irk you too? Living in beautiful Melbourne in country-of-the-future Australia?" I said.

"Yeah. She has a whole life thing going on out there too, mom," Campbell added.

India turned from the window and pointed toward the shoes she wanted Campbell to wear. "But she's not like Hamish. It's not nicey-nice with Marigold. For one thing she's always writing disturbing Op-Eds about melting glaciers and appearing in magazines without make-up, so she's hardly hidden away, and she's – what? Inept? Marigold can't irk you because she's Marigold, always pregnant and confused and – " India's voice trailed off, leaving the image of pregnant, confused, glacier-loving Marigold incomplete.

"*Hidden away*? Hamish lives in Paris, which is hardly hidden away. What's all this – whatever – about?" I asked. "It sounds borderline creepy."

Campbell jammed his feet into the shoes. "I love Ham, mom, and I'm not irked by him."

"Then why didn't *you* tell him we were coming?"

Campbell thought about that. "We don't talk. I mean, I don't write to him or anything. I suppose I could have called him. I would have, if I'd known you were keeping it a secret. Is it because of dad?"

India looked mystified, turning from me, (I had thrown Campbell's things from the chair and sat examining my nails), to Campbell, and back again.

"You know, the whole, whatever, between them?" Campbell attempted to clarify.

"Oh, good Lord, that's mostly mythology." She turned back to the window. "No, it's about me – about – everything that's been happening – " but again she left her thought incomplete.

Campbell looked at himself in the mirror on the back of the bathroom door. "Damn, but I'm a stud."

"Practicing your lines?" I asked. Then, "*Jestem cel meski mezcyzna*, says the translator app on my phone. I'm sure my pronunciation is atrocious."

"Indeed, it is," India said, "Polish is quite lovely, it sounds like rustling leaves; soothing. Maybe that's why it works so well for porn?"

"Do I irk you, mom?" Campbell said.

"No. You do not irk me, Campbell."

"So, I'm confused and inept like Marigold?"

"You're not inept, darling. You're very *ept*, in fact. Marigold certainly can't make her tits dance like you."

"That took practice."

"I'm sure," I said, winking at him.

"I've discussed this Hamish thing with my shrinks, of course," India said with a sigh. "I've told them I always feel like Lady Bracknell when I'm with Hamish. How can that be? How can you feel like Lady Bracknell when you're with your own son?"

"That lady from Oscar Wilde?"

"Yes, dear, that lady from Oscar Wilde."

Campbell shoved his wallet into his front pocket. "This is way deep, mom."

"Yes." India met his look with unexpected candour. "I suppose it is."

"Did I really ask you to marry me?" Campbell asked me.

"Ten years ago. The summer I turned twenty," I said. "You were skulking around the house for days afterward, afraid I might take you up on it and force you to make reservations at the Chateau Frontenac."

"Why would I ask that? I didn't want to get married at that age. I mean, I loved you and all, Justin, you know I did, but marriage? Why would I –"

"Just good fucking, I reckon," India said, giving her hair a fluff in the mirror. "Good fucking does that to twenty-somethings. Fortunately, evolution has trained most young people to ignore the silly things boys say in the moments before they ejaculate." She touched her watch. "Hurry on now, your father will be on his third Chardonnay at least and scribbling his next plot on cocktail napkins."

We had been seated at a banquet table on the side of the restaurant, next to floor-to-ceiling windows and the passers-by just a few feet away. Balfour – in his regulation blazer and tie – sat at one end of the table and India, in a stylish summer dress, at the other. Théophile, Campbell and I sat with our backs to the street. Javier, Nicolas, and Hamish faced us from across the wide table filled with bottles of mineral water and wine, plates, cutlery, flowers. Balfour had his right hand on Nicolas's arm (one of his favourite conversational postures), finishing his story about a serial killer in Wyoming who tried to copy the plot of his third novel. It contained its usual final flourish. "And now," he said, "they're making a TV movie about the guy copying my book. Art imitating life imitating art."

"We published that novel," Nicolas said. "*Cheveux sur le feu*. In fact, I settled upon this title. Not literal, of course, but quite good. No?"

"*We* published it?" Balfour asked, taken aback.

"My publishing house, yes. Our line of translations. Éditions de soleil? I remember reading about this man in the Wyoming. That man was very inspired by your book, Mr. Bedminster."

"Well – yes – apparently he was," Balfour said, still looking surprised by Nicolas's connection with the publishing world and – more importantly – Balfour's novel.

"At least we know it won't be a Hallmark Hall of Fame movie," I said.

"That must have been difficult for you, Mr. Bedminster. Did it give you writer's block?" Nicolas asked.

Balfour nodded sagely. Obviously, he'd been hoping for this kind of remark, thus he ignored my Hallmark quip, which he probably didn't understand (although he smiled). "Couldn't write a damn thing for – at least a month." He laughed loudly. "Okay, month and a half."

"Are you telling that worn-out old Wyoming story?" India waved from her end of the table.

"Just because you don't have any sculpture groupies in Wyoming." He said in riposte.

"How do you know? Perhaps I do. A whole cluster of them in – oh, dear, I can't think of a single city in Wyoming."

We all looked at one another in confusion.

"Cheyenne," Javier said. "Cheyenne is in Wyoming."

"There we are," India said. "I may have a huddle of groupies sculpting away out there in Cheyenne. Thank you, dear," she said to Javier. "Aren't you clever?"

The waiters brought our main courses and we began eating, speaking more quietly now to those sitting next to us.

"Why did you tell Hamish that I asked you to marry me?" Campbell asked me.

"I have no idea."

"What did you say?" Théophile asked from my other side.

"We're reminiscing," I said. "All those summers in the Bedminster / Chatterton house on Long Island. Hamish used to bring me home with him every summer, the ultimate tag-along."

"You were like another son," India said.

"There's a scary thought," Campbell said.

"How's Marigold?" I asked India.

"Same as always: overrun with infants and car seats and school reports and whooping cough and impetigo and – *that's* how Marigold is. My updates from down under are always the same, I'm afraid."

"Five kids must be a handful."

"Tell me about it. I'll expect her breasts to be sagging to her knees next time I see her."

Meanwhile, Nicolas had turned to Javier to tell him that he watched him that morning on television.

"You're not eating," India told me, pointing at my plate with her fork. "What's the matter?"

"I am too eating."

India watched me a moment. "You're not, you're trying to listen to," and she gestured. "What's his name down there."

"Nicolas. I want to be sure he has an enjoyable time."

"Hardly your responsibility, Poppet, and he's eating everything but the porcelain. Let's assume he's having an enjoyable time."

"Are you having a good time, Nicolas?" Hamish asked, having overheard India's remarks.

I'd been staring at Nicolas, admiring from a distance the way he spoke so casually, without affectation, so very masculine; he intrigued me.

"Why shouldn't he be having an enjoyable time?" Théophile asked.

"Yes, wonderful. Thanks," Nicolas said.

"You've got such long fingers. Do you play the piano?" I asked him.

"When I was young, yes. But not now." Nicolas looked at his fingers a moment. "The racquetball, but no piano."

"They're nice fingers," Hamish said.

"*Maigre*. Skinny? I am always being able to fish things out – that is the expression, yes? – from behind the sofa and between railings." He looked again at his fingers. "Handy to have such long fingers for holding the *raquette* – during racket-ball."

"Did you go running today in Luxembourg Gardens?" Théophile asked Campbell.

"Yes."

"Shirt off and hirsute Pecs doing their Texas two-step, I suspect," India said.

"As I listened to Madonna on my phone," Campbell shrugged genially. "And I always take my shirt off when I run, mom. It helps you get noticed. I pick up a boatload of guys that way."

India looked at me and sighed.

I loved India's confidence-sharing sigh, however shallow it might be. It felt maternal. Although Hamish's family appeared chaotic – even bizarre at times – they loved one another. My own family did not love one another; they did not even love themselves. My Uncle Irwin committed suicide by self-immo-lation at a shopping mall in Costa Mesa, in full view of a skating class on the ice rink. My sister Gillian dropped out of Stanford, had been in and out of drug rehab and lived now on a farm on up-country Maui with an (admittedly handsome) ex-Mormon with a Swastika tattoo. They raised goats and sold cheese, yoghurt and other reprehensible products. No doubt, they attended pro-Trump rallies in their free time. However, since she home-schooled their three boys, I doubted that be-tween teaching, milking goats and doing whatever yoghurt and cheese required that she had much free time for rallies.

I had always wanted to belong in Hamish's family, at-tached to someone as cool as Campbell – who wrote a poem one afternoon in a Greenwich Village Starbucks (the one across from the now demolished St. Vincent's Hospital), which his boyfriend *du jour*, who worked for *The New Yorker*, got published. In my family, a poem in *The New Yorker* would have merited everyone buying fifty copies and framing the page. In Hamish's family, no one mentioned it; when I told Campbell that I'd read it, he shrugged and said, "Whatever. I'm not dating Kurt anymore." The poem and the boyfriend were historically connected. I loved that. I glanced at India and Campbell. A wave of quivery emotion rolled over me. I felt a developing headache, worse than a headache, a something – which I recognized by now as the thing that had followed me since the Bataclan evening. Slyly I took my reserve Xanax from my shirt pocket and – when all eyes turned elsewhere – I slithered it down my throat.

"So," Balfour announced to the table, in his being-inter-viewed-on-The-Today-Show voice. "My book signing is to-morrow. You're all welcome to attend."

"A book signing?" Campbell said. "What would we do there? Stand around and watch you sign books?"

"I believe he does a little reading first," India said.

"Yes. I do. And I can reserve seats in the front for guests."

"Wonderful," Nicolas said. "I would prefer the front to our group seats."

Balfour looked at him thoughtfully.

"We always have the group seats," Nicolas said, "But this sounds much better, of course."

"I should work late tomorrow," Théophile said, though he hardly sounded disappointed. "However, if I miss the reading I'll see you at Justin's party."

"I'll come," I said. "Why the Hell not? Ham?"

Hamish dithered a moment too long, his eyes darting be-tween his parents, then he nodded and said, "Sure, of course." He looked sidewise at Javier, who had not yet declared himself.

In fact, Javier seemed to have no intention of saying any-thing. He calmly picked up his glass of water and drank from it.

"Right, then," Balfour said, still in his "Today Show" voice. "A toast." He held up his wine glass and everyone followed his lead. "To old friends, new friends – and to Justin, the almost birthday-boy."

We all toasted and drank.

I met Hamish's eyes across the table and I leaned toward India, drawing her in. "I'd have killed him if he'd said the word 'thirty."

"*Really?* Copy the method in one of his books then, like the serial killer in Wyoming," India said. "Balfour's got sev-eral viable scenarios, though I'm not sure where you'd buy a chain-saw in Paris."

"BHV," Hamish said. "In the basement. BHV has everything."

"Superb. Best get some battery acid too. Do they sell that separately? Perhaps you must buy the entire big car battery and drain it? They'll soon be outdated and unavailable since everything's going hybrid or electric, so best stock up. I don't think lithium batteries contain acid, do they? They merely explode and burn through people's trousers or set luggage compartments ablaze on aeroplanes. But never mind that," she said with an inexplicably deep sigh. "As I say, there are several viable murder scenarios to choose from – trust me, I've done my homework on murder scenarios. I may test one out myself."

Having finally finished dinner, we meandered down Boulevard Raspail in the general direction of the Hotel where India insisted she wanted an after-dinner drink. She had a recurring story about youthful trips to Paris with her parents, when they stayed in suites with balconies looking on the Eiffel Tower and the gilded *Les Invalides*. Our group stretched down the pavement in bunches, Balfour and India in the lead. At the moment, I walked with Nicolas on one side and Théophile on the other.

"Do we have an accurate head count for the party?" I asked Théophile.

He made his Gallic shrug. "Does it matter?"

"Doesn't it?"

"Not at all."

"How does that work, pray tell?"

"You order the food and servers; they put it out in the dining room and stand there to pour champagne. You make sure people know they can go anywhere –"

"Including the courtyard? That's always a problem, especially when you invite Americans."

Nicolas looked at me. "Why are Americans a problem in the courtyard?"

"Because they stand out there with drinks in their hands talking, and it just isn't done. Voices echo. The courtyard is for – what *is* the courtyard for?"

"Air and light," Nicolas said. "*L'architecture traditionnelle.*"

"Ask my mother, if you don't believe me," Théophile continued. "You don't need to know the number – people will come and go anyway, the early ones, the late ones, the stay forever ones like Hamish."

"And me," Nicolas said. "I never know how to judge when it is time to leave. I need the host to throw me out."

"That can be arranged," Théophile said.

"It sounds like a Charles Dickens' novel," I offered – since it did.

"Then we will need implausible coincidences and inopportune encounters," Nicolas said. "I adore *Great Expectations.* I read it at the Lycée, when I was preparing for the BAC."

"Then who's going to burn up like Miss Havisham?" I asked. "That's one of the best scenes in fiction, Miss Havisham catching fire in the wedding dress she's been wearing for years, going up like a bonfire and dying. Good stuff, death scenes. I swear Havisham must have inspired Balfour. You know, that scene in *Market Town Winter?* Let's ask him. Although no doubt he drew on the inspiration of my Uncle Irwin."

"I do not understand," Nicolas said.

"My Uncle self-immolated."

Nicolas shivered. "He burned up himself?"

"On a skating rink," I said. "He was very thorough, sat down on a pile of fireplace logs and then drenched them and him in gasoline. They had to use his teeth to identify him. As I recall, he had great teeth. I think he might have been protesting something, but I forget that part. My sister was always protesting things. Mind you, hearing about Uncle Irwin's immolation was not as bad as watching my mother get beheaded right in front of my eyes."

Nicolas looked at me in shock; while he knew about my condition, about Didier and Benoît's deaths at the Bataclan, clearly no one had told him about my mother. He continued to look intently at me, with his assessing, gentle gaze.

"A loose roofing slate. They have sharp edges." I shrugged. "Really, it's no wonder I'm a medicated basket case. My life is like a Stephen King or Balfour Bedminster novel. I'm a living horror story."

We were all three awkwardly quiet.

"Honestly," I said, looking at Nicolas rather than Théophile, "I often wonder what's next. A dirty bomb in the métro? A *Camion* running over people outside Luxembourg Garden? It boggles the mind."

"*On croit rêver*," Théophile told Nicolas, in response to me saying 'boggles.' "One of those bewildering Anglo-Saxon words to which one never gets accustomed."

"Like a roof slate beheading your mother," I said. "One of those strange French things to which one never gets accustomed."

3

The groups had shifted as we strolled and I walked now with Campbell.

"Théophile and I are having a rough patch, Campbell."

"Oh, man. Sorry."

"I don't think it demands a 'sorry,' it's just – well, I guess, I'm –" Campbell waited.

"I guess I needed something more from him – or maybe I never properly opened up to him about my feelings. But that's *never* been what our marriage was about. We've never really talked about – well, I don't know. I mean, I used my face and tight little butt to catch him and keep him. He didn't marry me to watch me cry and throw up and faint in public and pace the floor and look miserable. I'm no longer the Hugo Boss accessory he can take to parties in the fashionable suburbs."

Campbell slowed his pace and I felt him looking at me. "You know, I wonder if Théophile writing to my mom is about you; I doubt he's trying to be friends with her. He's probably been asking for help, you know – in dealing with things."

I shrugged. That made sense, actually. I put one hand up on Campbell's shoulder and we walked like that, hips brushing. I wanted to tell him all about how I felt that ghastly night – it felt completely right to tell him. Instead, I leaned into his warmth and rested my head a moment on his shoulder. Across the street, a throng of Chinese tourists had decanted at a café. Their luxury coaches idled in the 'No Parking' zone by the entrance to the métro. The tourists spilled out of the interior of the café to the pavement and on to Boulevard Raspail. No one could get by them, so angry pedestrians barked as befuddled waiters attempted to assert order. A number 96 bus – Théophile and I once termed it the alpha among Parisian buses – dinged its bell as more snarl than tinkle, mere centimetres from over-dressed Chinese matrons. This tidal wave of Chinese visitors with their air of entitlement represented something profoundly new.

Years ago, American tourists infested Paris like romantic locusts. Now, Chinese tourists turned up everywhere, and in a peculiar, non-romantic fashion, travelling in sleek buses in semi-disciplined groups, from one spot in the city to another, blowing through traffic lights with disdain. Presumably they hit all the tourist sites, but I only saw them in places such as this café or at a Pharmacy, where the shocked employees seemed utterly unprepared for an invasion of two hundred Mandarin-speaking customers. Then, as now, they filled the store, burst out the door to the pavement – and beyond.

"Do you suppose scouts travel ahead and plan these two-hundred swarm visits?" I asked Campbell.

"If so, then they're failing," he said.

Sometimes, I wondered if Parisians missed the old days of more solitary sojourners. I wasn't the only one who ducked down a side street when a troop of Chinese tourists approached, their uniformed, flag-carrying, megaphone-toting guide leading them. However, the French were quick to tell me – and anyone else – that China was the nation of the future and this was the century of China's rise, the more so since the election of an ignorant buffoon as American President. That alone proved America's days were numbered. Signs in Mandarin and Cantonese had now appeared in expensive shops, occasionally omitting English. Maybe that was the surest indication of the future? The French had always been fussy about signage.

"Something's forever lost in my life, Campbell."

He squeezed me and gave me a quick kiss on my neck. "You think too much, Justin. Just walk with me and be with me."

I snuggled still closer to him and thought that it might be good advice.

Clumped in over-stuffed *fauteuils*, we had taken over the lobby bar of the Hotel. I held a brandy, from which I sipped now and then, but mostly I just observed the scene. I sat Princess Diana-like. Long ago I had copied the way Diana held her legs, crossed at the ankles. I thought about telling our sex on the beach at Biarritz story or the time Théophile and I attended a wedding at a rented chateau in the Loire Valley and part of the ceiling collapsed during the reception. I had an extensive repertoire of party stories. But I simply sat with my Princess Diana legs attempting to look cute, sipping brandy, smiling at other peoples' stories. The hotel had a literary past and it prompted me to recall the last line from Hemingway's *The Sun also Rises*, when Jake Barnes and Brett Ashley are in the taxi and she says, 'Yes, wouldn't it be pretty to think so," or something like that.

"You're far away," Hamish said.

I turned to him. "I wish I were."

"You wish you were far away from Paris?"

"No. Just far away."

"I sort of get that," Hamish said. "The turning-thirty-mystical-phase."

"Is that an established phase, Doctor Freud? I presumed it was just my usual mix of diazepam and alcohol."

"For sure. It's like Fitzgerald. *This side of Paradise*? 'The last weird mystery; that held him with wild fascination and pounded his soul to flakes."

I felt myself recoil.

"Jesus, Justin. Are you all right?"

"I rather doubt it," I said cautiously. "Are you?"

Javier and I ran into one another in a hallway off the lobby, as we came out of the toilets. Holding up one hand, I managed to stop him as if I were a traffic cop. It worked. He paused in the middle of the corridor.

"Have I offended you?" I asked.

"Yes," he said.

"*Oh.*"

"But you offend a lot of people."

"*Excuse me?*" It had been my intention to sort a few things out with him, since I'd grown tired of his gruff and menacing presence, but this unexpected jab knocked me off my balance. I tried to conjure up a couple of angels for assistance, but it merely felt foolish and I felt my face grow hot as I blushed. "How have I offended you, Javier?"

"It's not something I'm discussing here in a hotel hallway," and he gestured toward the group in the bar.

I stared at him. "I don't think you like me."

"Is it a requirement?"

"Of –?"

"The sit around in the evening and drink group," he said.

I thought about the way he described us. "Of course not. It's just – aren't we supposed to be friends? Isn't that the idea of the thing?"

"The idea of what thing?"

"The idea of getting together every night."

"I haven't thought so," he said. "I am friends with Nicolas and Hamish, but not because we go to the café and drink too much. I could see them in other ways, at other times."

"You even see Hamish naked – in other ways, at other times."

He made a face.

"Why do you come at all then?"

"Why do you?" He asked. "When you have a husband at home?"

"My husband isn't any business of yours."

"Of course, he isn't. I don't know him. My question was about your behaviour, not about your husband."

I tried to look tough but felt nonplussed. "Just what the fuck have I done to you?"

"*Aha.* There you guys are," Hamish said, coming up to us at a trot, "Everyone's going his separate way. We're saying our goodbyes." He looked from one to the other. "Did I interrupt something here?"

"Don't be silly," I said, glaring at Javier.

"Yes," Javier said, putting his arm around Hamish's shoulder. "You did."

"How did we three, end up walking alone?" Hamish asked Balfour.

"And where are we going?" I said. "Did everyone else take the métro?"

"Nicolas and Théophile grabbed a taxi," Balfour said, "I think India went with them."

"But where'd Javier go?" Hamish asked. "He was right beside me on the way out."

"The good-looking plant guy who knows about Cheyenne, Wyoming?"

"My boyfriend."

"Who is good-looking, is a plant man and knows about Cheyenne, Wyoming?"

"Yes, dad." Hamish looked at Balfour and me. "Okay, this is just way weird," he said. Then seeing his father's expression, he added quickly, "Not that I mind."

"Are you trying to imitate a Seinfeld episode?"

"No."

"The correct answer was 'Yes, I am.'" Balfour clapped him on the back.

As always, events with Hamish's family had a Surrealist quality, rather like the hairy-chested gladiator angels I called up to the music of *The Rocky Horror Picture Show* as we walked – or at least I fantasized in that manner: A Dada-esque perambulation. We turned right and walked beside fashionable storefronts, peering into windows. Every now and then, we stopped to watch people walk by, tourists, Parisians, combinations of the two.

"Everyone says you hate me, Ham."

Although not directed at me, I felt Balfour's words like a blow to the stomach, another slug in this evening's bizarre boxing match.

"Jesus," Hamish said. "What a Hell of a thing to say."

"Why?" Balfour asked. "Everyone tells me you do."

"Everyone? Good God. They can't possibly. Of course, I don't hate you. I mean – *really, dad?*"

"Then why do I carry around this burden," Balfour said. "Why are there all these rumbling rumours about your disdain for me?"

We crossed the street and headed toward St. Sulpice Church, which I saw now in the distance.

"Maybe it's because I don't read your novels."

"Good Lord, there's a lot more to it than that," I said spontaneously.

Hamish gave me a curious almost-angry look; I shrugged.

"Look," Balfour said, "Are you still hung up about the decapitation?"

"No," Hamish said, glancing at me. I knew people avoided words like decapitation around me, not that they came up often in normal conversations. "I never read that book, so I was never hung up about it. I never said I was hung up about it. Mom was the one who tipped me off about the – head thing. No, I just – kind of like – you know, never read your books."

"So, if you come to the reading tomorrow, it'll be your first taste of my literary brew?" Balfour said.

"More or less."

"Methinks this is a rebellion against dad."

"*Methinks?*" I said.

Balfour smiled. "Shakespearean levity, Justin."

"Two things I can't imagine in any other family fight," I said, "Shakespeare or levity."

"We are not and never will be any other family, and you can thank India for that," Balfour said, though I couldn't tell if he meant it as compliment or complaint. "You obviously talk about not reading my books, with inappropriate interpellations. I'm your whipping boy. Must be. Otherwise, people wouldn't have reason to say you hate me."

"Who says that anyway? Mom?"

"Yes. And Marigold – and others."

We crossed over Rue de Rennes and paused by the Café Métro, where I came occasionally to flirt with a waiter named Romain. We stood looking at the conspicuously impressive vista, including the conspicuously handsome soldiers with their long guns, perhaps the only advantage to the prolonged state of emergency. We looked north then toward the heart of St. Germain de Près, with its lit façades and ancient church and the Café de Flore, its two broad terraces of literary-minded tourists just visible, a colourful marquee. The trendy storefronts flitted up the street. On the west side of Rue de Rennes, movie theatres emptied out. People scurried toward the métro or walked slowly off along the boulevard.

"I talk about it, sure," Hamish said. "I mean, I talk about not reading your books. But I don't think you're my whipping boy. Are we using that expression correctly? Doesn't it mean scapegoat?"

"Yes," Balfour said. "And yes. What you say about not reading my books makes Marigold – let's stick with Marigold for the moment. "

"Why?" I wondered.

"She's neutral, generally anyway."

"Is neutral a good thing?"

"Has been for Switzerland – or it was until they fell for that EU tomfoolery."

"If I'm a Seinfeld episode, what's that?" Hamish said. "Abbott and Costello?"

"More Mel Brooks," Balfour offered. "Back in the day. Look. What you say about not reading my books makes Marigold believe you hate me." He put a hand on Hamish's shoulder. "What in Christ's name do you say, anyway?"

Hamish looked askance at his father's hand. "I don't say much at all. We just don't get along very well, Dad. We never have."

"Never is a long time. Haven't we really?"

"No," Hamish said. "This is the first time we've talked in – God, years and years, since something like Christmas five years ago. Maybe since Justin's Uncle Irwin self-immolated on the skating rink. And tonight, is by accident, which is no doubt why you seized the moment to torment me."

"Oh, by the way, I know it sounds gruesome and a bit random," I said, "but I'm curious about something. Do you happen to know if my Uncle Irwin left his glasses on when he did it?"

"I never thought to ask," Balfour said. "Why?"

"Because he wore those hard-plastic horn rims. The idea of them melting has always haunted me."

"Poor Irwin."

"Poor children in the skating class," I said.

"Oh, them too, of course," Balfour said equably. "But it took balls to burn yourself up like that." He shook his head and removed his hand from Hamish's shoulder. "That Irwin. So, look, Hamish: Families often do quite well without talking to each other. But they don't have to trash one another."

Hamish looked at his father; Balfour looked back.

"I don't think I've ever trashed you, dad – even if Marigold did tell you I hate you."

Balfour hesitated. He shook his head. "Perhaps she never used the word hate."

We were all three quiet together a moment, then started walking again, onward toward St. Sulpice. None of us spoke until we were across the street from the fountain in front of the church. Although the church dominated our vision, with the tree-shaded shops to the left, light falling on the poster of an underwear model in a bulging red jock strap provided the Parisian context. People nervously ate at outdoor restaurants, looking prepared to sprint for the alley or dive to the floor at the first hint of mischief. Their talk drifted across Place St. Sulpice. Several equally apprehensive, gun-toting soldiers lingered where Rue Palatine jutted across the top of the square.

"Bigger interior than Notre Dame," Balfour said, pointing at the church.

"But it has that funky Delacroix painting," I said, "which isn't very good, and the towers don't match. What's that about?"

"I can't just suddenly explain how I've felt all these years," Hamish said. "It just isn't – you know – explainable."

"These family dynamic things – it isn't easy to give reasons for them," I said. "I agree with Ham. Although, I guess that if I've learned anything about families it's that they're are all dysfunctional in their own way."

"Positively Tolstoian, Justin, my lad," Balfour said. "Look, I understand more than I'm letting on. I'm an arrogant son-of-a-bitch, and insecure to boot. That's the worst combination, apparently. India has given me at least twenty books on the subject. So, I'm an asshole – fair enough. If I weren't me I don't think I'd like me much either."

"Campbell likes you," I said.

This took Balfour aback.

"Campbell likes everyone," Hamish said.

"Not anyone connected to Donald Trump," I said.

"Them excluded," Hamish agreed.

"I heard you didn't know we were coming over here for your birthday?" Balfour said to me. "Is that true?"

"Yes," I said. "It was a gigantic conspiracy of silence."

"*Hmm.* We were invited – by you, no less – so, I think gigantic conspiracy of silence is Trumpian hyperbole, don't you? Though if you sent it out as a tweet you would have to misspell both gigantic and conspiracy, at least on the first go around. India meant it as a happy surprise, no doubt." Balfour gave me one of his male-bonding claps on the back. "If it's any consolation, Ham, you and I weren't talking long before I came up with that decapitation plot. Though it's still a bestseller and we made a killing off the film rights, pun completely intended, and sorry about the beheading reference, Justin."

"No worries. Why *are* those two spires so weird?" I asked, as we crossed the street and walked toward the façade of St. Sulpice.

"Beats me," Balfour said.

India and I wandered listlessly around the Bon Marché department store. I couldn't tell if she really browsed the over-priced homewares or merely pretended. Could she possibly be interested in buying towels? What would she do, buy a set and stuff them into her suitcases? Nonetheless, ridiculous as it felt, I continued to saunter around the Descamps section with her – dutifully touching the towels, as India, feeling their thickness, exclaimed over the colours. Some dark blue ones appealed to her.

"These would make a wonderful gift for Campbell," she said.

"Towels?"

"Yes. I suspect Campbell does not have nice towels."

I felt momentarily dizzy. "Have you ever bought towels?" I asked since India held them as if they were Pashminas.

"I can't recall. How odd. Where did they all come from? They couldn't just have appeared in the linen closets by magic."

"A housekeeper?"

"Yes, no doubt," she said with a sigh, "I dry my most in-timate body parts on cotton chosen by hired help. You know, Justin, I've been considering a transition from sculpture to multi-media or mixed media."

"Which is it? Aren't they different?"

"Well, mastering the terminology would certainly be step one, I admit. I can't remember if I told Hamish, but in March,

I went to an impressive show at MoMA and was dazzled and enjealoused by Mike Kelley's Missing Time Colour Exercise No.2, and something – the name of which escapes me, but it was brilliantly bizarre – by Jim Lambie. These patches of colour and insertions of posters, seem cutting edge, cool and – well, doable, a new route to change."

"But why do you need to change?" I asked while examining my hair in a window.

"Because I have to change or become outmoded. I have a horror of becoming superfluous. Besides, being a famous sculptor doesn't really – *what?* Open doors, does it?"

"What doors do you need opened?" I said. "I mean, famous is famous. And you have groupies – even in Wyoming, as you pointed out."

"By the way, I recalled later that Jackson Hole is in Wyoming; I'm much more likely to have groupies in Jackson Hole than Cheyenne. But wherever they are, they're finite in number."

"Okay."

"Justin, don't take a tone. I'm not demented. I've thought about this a great deal. Most people only consider sculpture by accident – because a city planning ordinance made a big box store put something in front of their building – or by dint of herd mentality, like going to the Hôtel Biron to see Rodin's *The Thinker*. Is that what it's called in French? *Le Penseur?*"

"Yes," I said.

"I must become someone else." She sighed again. "Of course, multi-media art isn't a sure route to greater fame. But it gets bigger splash in Chelsea galleries and better press in the publications that count. Considering I already have a reputation – you can find India Chatterton in art books and Art History classes – I don't have to be great. I could get by with relative mediocrity for a while. My reputation could be like training wheels for my transformation."

"Not if you became someone else." I noticed beads of perspiration on India's forehead. "India, is everything all right?"

"Absolutely not. A period of profound anxiety is extremely difficult, as well you know, the more so since it seems ever more impervious to Xanax or clonazepam. Shouldn't it be more easily tamed?"

"I thought Xanax and a swig of vodka could cure anything."

"Well, it can't," India said. "I've tried that one. Really, have we come no farther than this since van Gogh was driven to cut off his own ear and poor Heath Ledger and Carrie Fisher met untimely ends? Apparently not. And my shrink – who should have all the answers – is worthless, though exceedingly handsome – you'd love him, Justin, trust me. He's your type. Don't you agree that it's more exciting to talk to a gorgeous young man named Judah with sexy sideburns than finding someone competent?"

"More exciting, for sure," I said, thinking of my own pasty-faced, doughy psychiatrist. "Does he have a hairy chest?"

"A pelt like a 70s shag carpet. He's superb. But perhaps my artistic crisis is more difficult because people think I'm hard and self-confident. There was that ridiculous televised middle-finger incident, which gave me more fame than my sculpture ever will. Good-looking-hairy-sideburn shrink Judah mentioned it first thing. Anyway, since people see me as this feisty woman of wonder, it complicates my ability to puzzle out my self-doubt. I can't phone someone up and say, 'Listen, Anne, I had an anxiety attack today on the corner of 20th Street and 6th Avenue.' She'd think it was a joke; she'd laugh."

We paused in front of yet another assortment of brightly coloured towels. How such discordant colours could look pleasing together intrigued me. I watched as India fiddled in her purse, found several Xanax and swallowed them. Well-practiced in the sly manoeuvres of pill swallowing, I had seen it coming.

"It galls me that Balfour," India said, "keeps getting ever more famous. His oeuvre is not artful; mine is. Yet Balfour Bedminster is known in the smallest outback towns, to troglodyte inhabitants of Texan cities where people still eat processed cheese spread, and to urbane multi-ethnic Manhattanites with a taste for the finest French wine. Nothing I do will ever reap Balfour's fame."

I held two towels up together, a fuchsia face towel and a purple bath towel. "Who in the Hell designed these?"

India snatched them from me and pushed them away, toward the back of the shelf, and then she closed her eyes a moment. "Justin, the Xanax has yet to start working. I know you saw me pop them. Shouldn't they be available by now as liquid gels, considering the number of people who take them? The pharmaceuticals industry seems to be forever behind the curve, despite their craving for profits. I can feel sweat starting to dribble down my right side. I may faint."

"*Vous en desirez?*"

India and I wheeled around and considered the startled face of a Bon Marché sales woman. "*Puis-je avoir des –*" India said weakly, touching her hand against the stacks of brightly coloured towels.

Though still looking startled, the saleswoman – accustomed to the vagaries of tourists – quickly recovered. She adjusted her school-marmish glasses and said officiously, "*Oui, Madame, bien sûr. Vous en desirez combien?*"

"Oh, Hell, Justin, I really am purchasing towels. *Trois*," India said, thinking her way through a forest of thorny French words, "*de chaque genre de –* what's the word for towel?"

"*Serviette*," I said.

"*Serviette*? But doesn't mean napkin? Are they the same word? Oh, good Lord, *de ces choses-là, petit à grand. C'est bien?*" The woman moved toward the towels.

"This damned Xanax better do something soon," India said, fumbling around in her purse, finding her pocketbook, and handing the woman her Visa card. "*Est-ce que je peux regler avec –* "

The woman who – in a very French way – had decided first to realign the towels India had thrown around, looked at the extended Visa card. "Yes, Madame," she said in crisp, British-accented English. "Of course – and money as well. We accept all ordinary forms of payment."

"He just handed you his T-shirt?"

"Pealed it off and handed it to me. Here it is," I said, holding it up. "We were attempting to play handball, at which I totally suck, no surprise, and I told him how much I liked it and – *voila* – he simply pulled it over his head and handed it to me."

"Is he scrumptious?"

"More than I'd realized, that's for sure – he's hairy and muscled. It's like his surprise announcement about being only *actif*. Who knew?"

"Question is, why on God's green earth is he single?" Hamish asked. "He's the catch of –"

"The week, at least," I said, "Perhaps even the month. What are you waiting for?"

Hamish gave me one of his prudish looks. "Uh, Javier?"

"He hates me, by the way," I said.

"He *dislikes* you." Hamish said. "And I've never felt warmly embraced by Théophile, truth be told."

We were sitting at one of the tables in the open front windows of a Chinese restaurant on Rue Montfauçon. It counted as an almost-elegant venue. India and Balfour swore by the food. Everything played to type, of course – a film set for a Cantonese restaurant in Paris, replete with bubbling aquarium and baroque chairs. From my vantage point, I could see the Carrefour de l'Odeon. People went up and down the crowded stairway to Mabillon métro stop. A line of people had formed at the cash machine at the apex of the triangle formed by the union of Boulevard St. Germain and Rue de Four. As always, Café Mabillon – newly refurbished – had people waiting beneath the chestnut trees for tables to free up. For a few moments, I looked at the store adjacent to the métro station. It had always been an attractive store, even if they never had anything I wanted to buy.

"Is it my imagination," Hamish asked, referring to the music that played through the restaurant speakers, "or is that a faux Chinese-sounding version of *Que sera, sera*? That old Doris Day song?"

I listened. "Doris was apparently a big hit in old Hong Kong."

Hamish took the T-shirt from me and read the French handball championship words. "Exceedingly cool T-shirt. I presume Nicolas is letting you keep it?"

"That seemed to be the idea of the thing."

"Are you going to wash it, or would that ruin its value?"

"What do you think?"

Hamish gave me back the shirt. "If he gave it to you as his chum, then wash the Hell out of the smelly rag – but if he gave it to you because he's a hairy hunk of man who wants to tackle your bones, then keep it unwashed and sleep with it under your pillow."

"I'm officially off the market, as well you know, young man, and my medicinal cocktail ensures that I have no boners to tackle." I sighed, but not entirely in the pretend manner I intended. My libido rose and fell, and the scent of the shirt did cause it to rise. Its present domestic flatline had more to do with my inability to connect with Théophile than with the combination of Prozac, Wellbutrin, Prazosin, Gabapentin, Mirtazapine, Clonazepam, Lunesta, Topiramate and Xanax I swallowed daily. "Nicolas is a hairy hunk of man who happens to be my chum." I caught the waiter's attention and asked for a pichet of red wine. "I might self-immolate, Ham, despite my fear of fire. I'm that desperate. Do you know of any ice rinks in Paris?"

"Don't joke about such things," he said with a shiver.

I shrugged and we listened to a siren warble down Boulevard St. Germain. "I'm amid a life crisis and I unburden myself and you tell me to stop joking?" We were silent a long while. I pinged on my glassware and watched the fish in the aquarium; I detested fish in aquariums. "Are you really afraid of Théophile?" I asked.

"*What?*"

"A week or so ago you said he was spooky – or spookier than the Pope, something along those lines."

"I don't remember any of that. And I'm not afraid of him, it's just that – he's kind of – I mean, sure, I'm afraid of him – in a way, but I don't know what that has to do with the Pope?"

"The cross-dressing old creep. Would you have sex with him if he asked? Théophile, not the Pope."

"God no."

"Why not? He's gorgeous, he's hairy, he's tall, he's as dominant as a gorilla in the Congo."

"And he's your husband."

"Pooh. Gather ye rosebuds while ye may. Isn't that the line?"

"'Gather ye rosebuds while ye may, Old Time is still a-flying: And this same flower that smiles to-day, to-morrow will be dying.' And some people gather rosebuds when they should be cultivating their home garden."

"My adorable moralistical nerd," I said, and my eyes filled with tears, "Everything in my life has changed – but you." When I turned and looked out the window, my sense of ripening crisis only loomed larger. I saw my life stretched out before me like a flat plain; I glimpsed a horizon without discernible landmarks. My mouth tasted cottony with fear. I felt dazed; I felt worthless. A pair of birds, suddenly framed against the rooftops, drifted across the sky.

My coming out had become Beverly Hills folklore. As a rule, the wealthier set kept such events as family rough and tumble quiet – however, unfortunately for society, my family could never be quiet on any subject. I had chosen what I *thought* to be a perfect moment; we had eaten Christmas dinner, with aunt and uncle and sister, all together, sprawled about the living room soothingly liquored up.

However, the *Justin Situation* – as the Beverly Hills Country Club dubbed it – did not go as planned. In this as in so many things, my family marched to a drummer from a Doris Day and Rock Hudson film. Frankly a disgrace to the socially liberal if occasionally politically Neanderthal norms of Beverly Hills, they had yet to make the leap of understanding that gay equaled normal, let alone acknowledge – or begin to grasp—the urgent necessities of transgender men and women, such as my friend Roxanne (whom they never knew had started sixth grade as Randall). I made my short, eloquent announcement, briefly quoting from a book by Doctor Ruth

– and then my mother screamed in "*Rocky Horror Picture Show*
style" and fainted – although she crumpled into a suspiciously
comfortable position on a thick Persian carpet.

My father fired off curses, followed by launching my
tennis trophy through the living room window, roaring over
the smashing glass, "You won't want this anymore." I still don't
know what he meant by that, since I never liked the hideous
trophy, he did; and tennis is hardly Rugby or Football if he
aimed for an emasculation theme, while Djokovic, Federer and
Nadal all seem amply amped with heterosexual testosterone.
My uncle took a milder path – being a guest in the house and
not only more liberal but clearly imagining how it could help
his own son's college admission prospects to be able to write
about the horrors of gay oppression at the Century City West-
field Mall – of throwing his whiskey tumbler into the fireplace,
and shouting ridiculously, "He's a fine-looking young man and
a damn snappy dresser, but in the name of family unity we'll
support you until *Hell freezes over*." Considering my family,
odds are we'd know about that freezing-over sooner rather than
later.

For her part, my sister – while clapping her hands and pe-
riodically whistling with two fingers – leapt around the room,
over my mother and the broken glass from the window – through
which the tennis trophy had been projected – shrieking, "How
exciting, how amazing, oh, *wow*, my very own gay brother, isn't
this just *fantastic*, Muffin?" In the foggy beginnings of time, I
had earned the nickname Muffin. Various theories as to its origin had come and gone, but my mother remained ever furious
about people referring to her son by the same name, "As some
big haired woman's *Chihuahua*." For most of my youth, I trea-
sured my moniker. However, in close juxtaposition I moved
from having my first long-term Italian boyfriend screaming

shirtless from our fourth-floor window, "*Muffie-poo*," to living with a hunk of a Frenchman whose mouth could only say something that rhymed with Loofah, the French 'u' being one of those sounds foreigner's never master and Frenchmen never lose. Fortunately, Théophile proved more trainable than Paolo and we settled on Justin.

I've always had complete ambivalence about growing up in Southern California. I loathed and loved it in equal measure. Those hideous Christmas Eves when it hovered near 80 degrees and I longed for sleigh bells 'ringing and jing ting tingaling too,' scarfs, snow and frosty breath. I asked for a coat with a faux fur collar one year, and I swanned around wearing it, sweating and wishing I were in upstate Maine. Then again, we had such beautiful spring mornings – as in mid-February – alive with freshly watered lawns and gorgeous tight-shirted guys in shorts. I grew up with a bifurcated geographical flight or fight syndrome. I wanted to flee Eastward toward seasons and where people read books (and ultimately, I did); I wanted to stay and fight the good fight, savoring drives up Palm-tree lined Doheny Boulevard or lazy lunches on Rodeo Drive. I disliked the sun and had learned to slather on sunscreen in kindergarten, but I loved what the sun provided, that lavish spectacle of everything from hibiscus to Birds of Paradise, towering pines, jacarandas, pepper trees. As someone once said to me, "Plant it, water it, and it will grow." Jack and his beanstalk would have loved Beverly Hills.

Hamish lifted his face from the menu and met my wet eyes. "Everything is the same, Justin, and I'm not your – anything. You're probably fretting over your birthday. Thirty is just a number, and ageing is a process not a – well, not a whatever –"

"A destination? I think that's the cliché you're searching for, oh ye with claims to English teacher-hood. Though you did impress me with that poetry incantation." I shook my head and dried my eyes. "It's huge, what's happening to me – it's, what? Seismic?"

"*Seismic?* What do you mean what's happening to you? How is it seismic? I mean, you haven't even turned thirty yet."

"My life is ruined."

I felt Hamish's eyes on me like a medical examination.

"I'm sorry, Justin. I know things have been –"

We looked up as India came into the restaurant carrying two enormous Bon Marché shopping bags.

"What?" she said, catching the expression on Hamish's face. "They're towels, for Campbell. Justin and I found them at the Bon Marché and you know the French – they're perfect. Well, not the French, God forbid – the towels. I mean to say, the French have perfect design sense. Oh, bugger it – I don't know what the Hell I mean."

"Buy what you want, mom," Hamish said.

"I shall. I do. Campbell has nothing that matches. Now he will." Then catching the eye of the waiter, who recognized her from her last visit she said, "A glass of Montrachet, please. By the way," she told us, "as you may just have noticed, I'm not speaking French for the rest of the day."

"Why not?" Hamish asked.

"Because I'm not." Her glare brooked no compromise. "To be blunt, it just doesn't do to encourage them."

"Who?"

"The French, darling."

"But it's their country."

"Where's your father?" India looked over her shoulder, as if Balfour might be lurking by the fish aquarium.

"Was he invited?" Hamish asked.

"I thought so. Maybe not." She looked at me. "Was he?"

"We decided he was best off preparing for his reading and signing, or signing and reading," I said. "To which, in case you have any interest, Théophile is not coming. However, his mother is. She's driving up from the Vendée and staying at their apartment on Avenue Foch."

"You're kidding," Hamish said.

"When have I ever kidded about Théophile's mother?"

A fearsome aristocratic force of nature, Théophile's mother had driven us to our wedding from the family Chateau to the church, windows down, headset tied securely in place by a loop of twine, belting out the lyrics of Mylène Farmer's "*Elle a dit*." She had swerved on to the narrow highway shoulder, punched her Land Rover to 110 kilometres per hour, avoided a decomposed wheel rim, grazed the concrete barrier, and then rocketed in front of a hulking two-trailered Carrefour Super-market truck, all without missing a beat. Famed for knowing every means of dodging traffic jams, she frequently drove on the wrong side of the road, off-roaded through the back gardens of traumatized middle-class families, tore across fields and made death-defying treks through woodlands. Once, she made it across the tarmac of a rural airport in front of a plane, when it proved indispensable that she make it to a funeral – unfortunately, not her own.

"She'll sit next to me the whole time calling me "*vous*" in that old-fashioned voice of hers and critiquing my choice of clothes – which, in her view, won't be appropriate."

"Will they be?" India asked.

I reached for one of the prawn crackers and put some chili paste on it with a little spoon.

"Your clothes. Will they be appropriate?" she pursued.

"Yes, I heard you. I was pondering. Of course, they'll be appropriate. But not from her perspective. She goes by some absurdly archaic handbook of style from like – the Empress Eugènie."

"Perhaps," India said, "she's trying to be helpful."

"*Helpful?* The flesh-eating old bat? She hates me. She loathes the idea that I'll be at every significant family gathering until the day she dies – which will be decades, if she hasn't spontaneously combusted or been smashed by an A380 she's driven in front of before then. Isn't there a proven link between cases of spontaneous combustion and evil?"

India gave me a disapproving look, then sighed. "I don't know what the Hell Balfour has to prepare for? What would that entail? Soaking his wrist in ice? Presumably he's chosen the chapter he's reading."

"Aha, there's our boy," I said, waving at Campbell, who had appeared in the doorway.

"He's not wearing shorts, is he?" India asked.

"Chinos and an untucked dress shirt," I said, as Campbell came up to our table.

"Are you describing what I'm wearing?" he asked, pulling out a chair.

"Your mother was worried that you might be wearing shorts."

He sat down. "A lot of French guys wear shorts now in Paris. Things have changed, mother." He unbuttoned another button on his shirt. "It's getting hot."

"A *canicule* – a heat wave," India said. "It always kills thousands of old people, as if summer catches them by surprise. They were stacked like cordwood in refrigerated vans back in – what? Summer of 2003."

"What was stacked like cordwood?" Hamish asked.

"The dead old people. The refrigerator vans were parked over by the *Hôtel de Ville.*"

"Do you comb it?" I asked, touching my hand against Campbell's chest. "It's always so perfect your chest hair."

"No." Campbell looked down. "It's just naturally perfect chest hair. Like my teeth," and he flashed a snow-white smile.

"No one's teeth are naturally the colour of Sevrès porcelain," Hamish said. "The reflection could blind someone."

"Here," India said, pushing one of the bags toward him with her foot. "For you."

Campbell opened the top of one of the bags and looked in. "*Towels?* How the Hell am I supposed to get them home? My suitcase wouldn't fit another pair of socks, let alone – *Jesus, mom*. How the Hell many towels are there?"

"Three of each kind. And three face flannels."

"I'll have to buy another suitcase just for these." Campbell looked around the table. "That doesn't exactly make them a gift."

"Don't be ungrateful," India said. Then, "Thank God," as the waiter brought her wine. "I'm parched. Throw them out for all I care. It's the thought that counts, even with a three of everything towel collection. God forbid you should just accept them graciously. You are your father's son, Campbell." She held her fingers to her temples, as if she had a headache. "Why is there a handball championship T-shirt on your lap?" she asked me.

"It's his new sex toy," Hamish said, stealing a sip of India's wine.

4

"I need to talk," I said.

"But how did you know I was awake?" Théophile asked.

"Sleeping people make more noise. You haven't rustled your blanket, coughed, burped, or banged the pillow in half an hour."

"You've been listening to me think."

"Which is ever so much nicer than listening to you snore," I said. "Mostly."

"Why are we having this midnight vigil?"

I wondered about that. Why *was* Théophile lying there awake?

"Of course," Théophile said, sounding very French, "There is always too much to think about in today's world."

"True," I said. "In ten years the Seine shall be nipping at our street corner thanks to global warming."

"A hundred years, perhaps."

"In earth terms," I said, "There is no difference."

'It's often seems as if there is more to *avoid* thinking about than actually to think about."

I reflected on that. Théophile, like India, seemed – *what?* Different? Changed or changing? Something. "You hurt my feelings tonight," I said, touching upon a discussion we had while getting ready for bed. "You gave me *that look*."

"Yes, I know your feelings were hurt. As you listened to me think, I've been listening to you brood."

"But I don't hear an apology."

"As you know, some of the best moments in my life have been apologies," Théophile said, which struck me as a mystifying remark. Could that possibly be true? "I did not hurt your feelings on purpose; it was a domestic tiff."

I reached over and swirled my fingers in Théophile's chest hair. Why did you fall in love with me?"

"It happened. There was not one reason."

This sounded accurate and quite French. "Do you remember when we watched the old version of *Far from the Madding Crowd*?"

"Yes," Théophile said.

"I loved when Sergeant Troy pried open Fanny's coffin and found the baby. I remember thinking Terence Stamp made a heavenly Sergeant Troy. That scene with the flashing swords? That penis symbolism. And I was obsessed with Julie Christie. If I ever do high camp, I'll be Julie Christie."

"You haven't got the right hair."

"I'll get a wig."

"But why are we talking about this film?" Théophile asked.

"Because it's safer than talking about *real* things," I said sadly.

"There is no safety," Théophile said gently, "it's an illusion, something we conjure up, an attempt to give a fixed reference point within the chaos of existence. I'm certain your psychiatrist must have told you this. The thought of safety makes us feel better, but in the end, safety is illusory."

"Not always," I said. "And maybe those phantasms – safety, security, foreverness – are what life is all about? Maybe they are what is real."

"It's real that we're alive – and that we're all going to die," Théophile said.

"But death itself isn't real," I said, my voice rising, feeling perspiration beneath my hand on Théophile's chest, "It's something we only know *about*, we don't know it, we do not know what it *is*. I suspect there's a great deal more to dying than simply dying." Confused but stimulated by the contradictory turmoil of my thoughts, I put my head on Théophile's chest.

"Go to sleep, Cinderella," Théophile said. "You're turning into a pumpkin."

"The truth hurts," I said softly, thinking of Sergeant Troy and the horror of that open coffin.

"No more or less than lies," Théophile said.

We were awakened by the buzzer on our door and stared groggily at one another, puzzled, since anyone buzzing our door had to be a neighbour or someone in possession of multiple digi-codes. I heaved myself over the edge of the bed, put on a pair of boxers, found my slippers, and shuffled out to the living room. Opening the door, I studied the travel-weary face of Hamish's sister Marigold. We rushed into a hug, Marigold fumbling with a huge suitcase, until we could shut the door.

Théophile had appeared in his own pair of American-style boxer shorts. "Marigold," he said, giving her kisses on both cheeks.

"It's a complete fiasco," Marigold told us. "I've ruined the surprise. I was meant to phone Nicolas from the airport, but somewhere along my epic journey from down under I misplaced my phone, which Qantas *assures* me they'll locate – though I'm not sure how they know that. It's terrifying how little privacy we really have. Standing there at Charles de Gaulle, I couldn't remember anything except your address, that's how tired I am. It's bloody difficult traveling from our home to you northern hemisphere types, it's always one day before you left Australia or two days after. I can't imagine what it does to your body. Speaking of which," she said, as she collapsed on the sofa, turning even paler than when she arrived, "might I have several litres of water?"

As Théophile sprinted toward the kitchen, I observed Marigold, who retained her beauty; no drooping breasts or haggard stay-at-home mother shadows fell over her stylish figure. She looked like a young India and exuded a sense of cultured calm. Clearly, I underestimated the cosmopolitan chic of Melbourne.

"You're the last person I expected to find in our apartment this morning."

"Certainly not the last."

"Toward the bottom, at any rate. Are Gareth and the kids here too?"

"Blessedly no," she said. "They've been left to wreak havoc on the streets of Melbourne," she pronounced her home as Mel'bun. "I suspect it's ice lollies for breakfast and candy floss for dinner. No," she shook her head, "Gareth's a sport, he's happy watching over them for a few days." She must have been giving me an assessment because she announced, "It's done you all in, hasn't it, Justin?"

"It has, Marigold – it – well, it has."

She came to sit beside me, with an aroma of pricey perfume, and gave me a kiss on my forehead.

It felt odd being kissed in that manner by Marigold. Not condescending exactly, but not quite adult; I felt like a youngster who'd had a bad week at school. "Thanks for the emails – you know, the awareness of how hard it was – still is," and my voice quavered. "My friends –"

"I met them," Marigold said, "I remember how Didier teased me about my accent – and Benoît, well he was charming."

We both stared a moment across the room and out the windows, at the rooftops and windows of our neighbourhood.

"I'm ever so sorry," Marigold said.

We leaned our heads together; Théophile reappeared with a litre bottle of Wattwiller water, opened the top, and handed it to Marigold. She drank in long, quenching gulps.

"Someone had best phone Nicolas and tell him about my disaster," she said. "And then I need to get a taxi or car service to take me there. I *must* shower and rest."

"You're welcome to stay here," I said.

"Yes, of course," Théophile echoed.

With another, final swig of water, Marigold said, "It would be a bit mean of us to leave poor Nicolas in the lurch – the more so since he's been pining away for Hamish for so long."

"*What?*" I said.

"You doubt my psychic powers?"

"Yes," I said, "Or you would have warned me about – that night. Why do you think Nicolas is pining for Hamish? And isn't Javier rather in the way? And why would you being there make any difference?"

"Pooh. *Amor vincit omnia.* Our Hamish needs to get a move on and find someone with whom he can settle down. I can assist."

"Agreed on that, and despite the fact that we hate one another Javier would meet all settling down requirements. You'll see. But, honestly, I haven't had the slightest hint that Nicolas had an interest in Hamish – or vice versa."

She waved her hand, in the same fashion as India did. "I'll give young Nicolas some Hamish love tips."

"Like what? Be rough and tough and hard to please?"

"No, no, that's the sort of lunk that Ham chases and dumps when what he wants is someone like our mum: over-protective, loving to a fault, forgiving and a bit ditzy. Didn't some researcher conclude that gay men look for partners who remind them of their mothers?"

"Lord, what a *ghastly thought*," I said. "If Théophile chose me because I resemble his Gorgon of a mother, well – did you?"

"No," Théophile said, "You and my mother have nothing in common except your willingness to judge others unkindly and a tendency to be pretentious."

"I'm glad we cleared that up, then," I said, giving Théophile a harsh squint. "However, I see your point where Ham is concerned."

"You gave a fairly accurate description of Nicolas," Théophile said, "But, in fairness, also of Javier. Javier has much of India's strength of will."

"My God," Marigold said, "the two of you, you only get more handsome. You're a tad too thin, Justin, but still."

"I'm turning thirty," I moaned, "I live in fear of growing my father's tits."

"Those are relatively new and he said he's having a procedure," Théophile said.

"*Huh*. I'll wait and see. He has a fear of doctors – though that might be overridden by his greater fear of looking like Donald Trump in his Donald Duck golf gear."

Marigold stood up. "Now. Enough about elderly male breasts and Presidential rear ends the size of Fiats. Nicolas?"

"I'll phone him now," I said. "And I'll ride with you in the car; I've never seen Nicolas's apartment; a boy does like a good snoop."

We both laughed.

I knew Nicolas's address on Rue de Thann, but I'd forgotten how stylish the neighbourhood remained. I ogled the
ornate monuments that surrounded the Place Courcelles. Most
of the buildings – legacies of an era when social class bought
safety – still did not require a code to enter the main foyer;
Nicolas's lobby proved merely an elegant marbled drawbridge,
beyond which travel proved impossible. Marigold and I stared
at a set of metal and glass doors that sealed off the stairs and
elevator. A panel next to one door contained buzzers with a
blizzard of plastic, paper, tape and handwriting: buzzers with
double names, buzzers without names, names without buzzers.
On my third read-through, I finally discovered a button with
the faded name Perrault and pressed it.

"*Toutes les livraisons au gardien,*" Nicolas said through the
speaker.

"Nicolas?"

"*Oui.*"

"It's Justin and Marigold." A crackly moment of amazed
surprise. "I'd better bring her up before she faints."

"Yes, yes, of course. Come up, please – to the third floor, just
off the *ascenseur.*"

The buzzer sounded, I pushed open one of the glass doors,
and then we rode the *ascenseur* to the third floor where, as prom-
ised, Nicolas stood in an apartment doorway in a tight T-shirt.

"Good lord, you've got great pecs. What gym do you go to?"
Marigold asked.

"Are you familiar with Paris gyms?" I asked her.

I meant, you must go to the gym," She said. "I'm exhausted,
so excuse my lack of precision. Nicolas looked embarrassed. "At
the office, it's a perk of management."

He brought us into an apartment with planked wood
floors, high ceilings, chandeliers, fireplaces, velvet drapes, and

dramatic Second Empire furniture. I ran my hand along the back of a velvet sofa. The air smelled of vanilla.

"What a stunning apartment," Marigold said. "And I'm sorry about this morning, Nicolas. I lost my phone, somewhere – who knows? Well, Qantas, apparently. I could only remember Justin's address. I've ruined everything, haven't I?"

"No, no, of course not," Nicolas said. "I am certain it was a surprise nonetheless when you appeared at the door of Justin."

"Oh, it was," I said. "Trust me."

"This apartment is absolutely spectacular," Marigold said. "I'll feel as if I'm staying in the Élysée Palace."

"Very different from that but thank you. It is my grandmother's, though she lives now in Biarritz."

I had gone to one of the sets of *portes fenêtres* that looked down on the graceful faces of Rue de Thann. When I turned around, Marigold had collapsed in an armchair and Nicolas lazily stretched his arms over his head.

"You look quite good for someone who has traversed the globe," Nicolas told Marigold.

"Not worn down from child bearing?" she laughed.

"Excuse me?"

"Sorry. A family joke."

"*Yes?*" he said, clearly confused.

Marigold put her hand on a porcelain bowl. She turned it over and examined the markings. "Gracious. This is genuine Meissen. I thought it might be."

"A gift to me from Margaret Drabble," Nicolas told her.

"*Was it really?*" Marigold said. "I mean – *really*? She's one of the best writers in the English language. I absolutely adore *Jerusalem the Golden*. Do you know it?"

"But of course," he said.

They looked at one another for a long time. Watching them, I felt myself to be in the presence of sophisticated people

– something rare and something with which I rarely felt at ease. I had married Théophile as much for his money and the access it gave me to high culture and sophistication as I did for his hunky good looks. I had dropped my then boyfriend Paolo the day after I met Théophile, even though Paolo's lovemaking had given me such a thrill that I still tingled when remembering our passion; but passionate Paolo, poor as a church mouse, offered nothing but good sex. Yet, as safe, secure and – *yes* – sophisticated as life became with Théophile, it had yet to make me at ease in the ethereal refinement of Marigold, India, Campbell, and Hamish, all of whose DNA had been encoded for culture. Money can't buy everything, it's true; but what it can't buy is precisely what I could most have used.

Théophile, Nicolas, Marigold and Campbell *always* wore the proper shoes to the proper venue. How they knew that mystified me. It wasn't learnable; I'd tried. I couldn't imitate either Théophile or the models in *Sense and Sensibility* beyond a certain monkey-see, monkey-do level. Like Margaret Thatcher, about whom I had read recently, the aristocracy would always identify me as an interloper by those slips in pronunciation, my *faux pas* in *prêt-à-porter* outfits. I wasn't as obviously a misfit as someone like Donald Trump, God forbid, but I had yet to decipher the code. Perhaps Théophile had been a poor teacher? Had he even tried? I wasn't sure he'd given much effort to teaching me my aristocratic rites of initiation. Marigold exuded her self-confident self-awareness and Nicolas, with his grizzled chin, a sense of independence; perhaps, I thought, the small aspects of social grace mattered most? Perhaps mastering those would be the first step in my initiation? I looked again at the two of them. Perhaps, I thought; *perhaps*.

"Some coffee or tea?" Nicolas asked us.

"Coffee, please," Marigold said.

"This way." Nicolas inclined his head and we followed him down a panelled corridor to a kitchen overlooking the courtyard. Through another door, I saw a velvet-curtained dining room. Nicolas motioned for us to sit as he began moving about, filling a coffee press with coarsely ground coffee, heating the water in a kettle – did the kitchen even have a microwave? I didn't see one – then pouring the water, which must already have been hot because it burst into steam in minutes, over the grounds. As the coffee infused, he asked Marigold, with another lazy scratch of his chest and stretch of his arms, "Perhaps you wouldn't rather I show you to your room? You must need a good, long sleep."

"A quick cuppa, then yes, I'll sleep for hours, Nicolas."

As he poured our coffee, Marigold rumpled his hair and asked, "So, how long have you been in love with my brother?"

They were speaking in English, so it took Nicolas a moment to process her use of the word love, then he blushed and put some honey on his croissant. "There has been some mistake. I am not in love with your brother."

"Are you just being bashful?"

Nicolas shook his head, popping a piece of the croissant in his mouth and washing it down with coffee. "Again, I am afraid there has been some mistake. Does Hamish report this?"

"No, no, not at all," Marigold said. "I have believed it to be true. I'm psychic. And you're – well, I'll give you the best compliment I can, Nicolas: you remind me of my husband Gareth. Hamish would be *bound* to be attracted to you."

"Oh, Gareth," Nicolas said, still flushed, but with a wink at me, "The potent Gareth who exports his sperm and has black chest hair."

Marigold nearly choked on her coffee. "Exports his *what*?"

"I understood from Justin that he was bestselling in the sperm banks and his sperms are exported to China and Sweden."

Marigold burst out laughing and waved a dismissive hand in my direction.

"He was telling us about how you and Gareth met in South Africa and then moved to Australia."

"I see," Marigold said, looking at me. "Justin and my mother enjoy making my life into a wilder drama than ever it really was – *or is*. I'm flattered that you thought Gareth's semen export-worthy, Justin, though I'm not about to allow it. I have a monopoly on that product."

"And indeed, you've used it well." I sipped my coffee with a shrug. "It was merely idle speculation. Gareth is the sort of man about whom troops of gay men are bound to speculate idly."

"Is he really? I'll tell him," Marigold said. "He'll preen next time we're in Collingwood." She finished her coffee and, brushing back her hair motioned toward her suitcase. "I think I'll take you up on that chance to sleep now, Nicolas. I feel a tad woozy."

"But, of course," Nicolas said, managing to get her on one arm and the suitcase tucked under the other and then he had them trundling down a corridor.

I stood up and went to the windows, looking down on the elegant, orderly courtyard.

Nicolas's hand fell on my shoulder, squeezing it with the certain comfort of friendship.

"Thank you for arranging Marigold's visit as a surprise for me, Nicolas. It's a wonderful gift."

"We all thought it would please you."

I heard a clock ticking in the dining room. "Really, Nicolas, this apartment is amazing. You live here with your sister the judge?"

"Yes. She is out shopping. Moreover, we have three cats living with us: Sister Sledge, Elodie, after Elodie Frege, and Tina, after –"

"Tina Turner?"

"Or Tina Arena."

"A trio of very gay cats."

"Yes. I think they are hunting in the courtyard somewhere. They stick together *ces trois félins criminels*. Justin?"

"Yes?"

"Your hand is shaking. Are you feeling ill?"

"It's just anxiety – well, *just anxiety*, who would ever have thought I would be saying that? Everything is spinning around and around, Nicolas. Something about Marigold's arrival maybe, and – something's terribly wrong between me and Théophile. I think too much about – about that night, and I'm worried that something's changed fundamentally between Théophile and me. *Has it?* Does he still love me? Do I still love him? Everything's out of focus. I feel sometimes as if my life is all wrong, as if I need to," and I surprised myself by saying, "start fresh."

"You have so much pain," Nicolas said.

"Pain," I said, with that growing sense of doom that precedes a panic attack. "Do you suppose Théophile still loves me? He's so distant, so – perfunctory. Does he? Love me? Am I unlovable now?"

"You are not unlovable, Justin, quite the contrary. But here, here," he said, helping me to sit down. "Let's phone Théophile – though not for these reasons."

I liked the comforting pressure of Nicolas's strong hand on my neck. I wanted *this* from Théophile; love felt like this.

"Let's have him come and fetch you," Nicolas said. "Yes?"

"Holy freaking Mother of God," I said to Hamish. "Look at my face, so you can tell people what I looked like in the moments before my fatal stroke."

"*What?*"

"That's what," I said, pointing to where Théophile and Campbell had just entered the Café.

Campbell garnered a Richter-scale level of ogling. Heads swiveled; friends nudged friends. Even the bartender – the cute one with the barbed wire tattoo on his upper arm – stopped drawing a beer to stare. Théophile and Campbell made their way toward our table.

"We thought we'd find you here," Campbell said.

"We *knew* we would find you here," Théophile clarified.

They pulled up chairs.

"I'm going to the reading," Campbell said, then to the waiter who materialized – miraculously by the standards of the café – at his side, "A beer, please."

"I'm going home," Théophile said. "Though I may go for dinner in Neuilly. In any case, I am certainly not going to the reading."

"I haven't decided yet if I'm going," Hamish said.

"Do it," Campbell said, putting his hand on Hamish's back.

"Thanks, Campbell. Very motivational."

"I absolutely, positively cannot believe you're here," I said to Théophile. "Really. I'm blown away by this."

Théophile looked around. "Aren't many others here in a suit."

"The suit is not the issue."

"I'm sure they imagine I am one of them."

"*Hardly*," I said. "You reek of straight."

"I don't think it is as cut and dry – dry or dried? – as that," Théophile said.

"Dried," Hamish said. "Cut and dried."

"Believe me. You're the poster boy for straight. Not a soul here would think you were gay." I drew my hand over the crowded room.

"You are right, though. It's not really regulation wear," Hamish told Théophile, touching his suit lapel. "Nicolas gets away with it. But, of course, he's Nicolas, so – you know. Jesus, *you're certainly a hit*," he said to Campbell.

"I caught that," Campbell said.

"It's because he looks like a Roman god – or an American marine out of uniform. Why *are* you two here?" I asked.

"It was my idea," Campbell said. "We were having some coffee up in La Defense and –"

"The two of you?" I said.

"Yes."

"Alone?" I asked, nearly as startled as I'd been by seeing them walk into the café.

"Yes."

"I just don't see what the two of you – I mean, why on earth would you want to have coffee with Campbell? No offense, Campbell."

"But I take offense," Campbell said and emotion abruptly shadowed his handsome face. He looked at me in an ephemeral explosion of feeling, before lowering his eyes to the table and extinguishing his sensitivities. "Théophile needed to share something, and it's not like it's the first time the two of us have met up with each other. We have things in common."

"Like what?" I demanded.

Campbell and Théophile exchanged a look, which mystified and irked me in equal measure. They kept secrets from me now?

"I wonder where Javier is?" Hamish asked.

"I'm guessing wherever he wants to be," I said, still wondering why Théophile would want to talk to Campbell? They were the most unlikely of confidants.

Nicolas, satchel over one shoulder and suit jacket over an arm, came toward us.

"Have you seen Javier?" Hamish asked.

"Why should I have seen him?" Nicolas asked, sitting on the chair Théophile turned around for him from another table, and trying unsuccessfully to get the attention of the waiter.

"Here," Campbell said, "let me help you." He held up his hand and the waiter appeared at our table. "I think we need some more drinks here."

"*Un pastis*," Théophile said.

"*Une bière*," Nicolas said.

"Where is he?" Hamish said. "He hasn't phoned or answered my texts?"

Nicolas shrugged, causing his satchel to crash to the floor.

"This is not such a bad place," Théophile said, looking around again, and this time catching someone's eye. "Not bad at all."

"Oh, good Lord," I said. "Has everyone lost their mind?"

"His or her mind," Hamish clarified.

"Thank you, professor," I said with practiced sarcasm, and making a good imitation of a schoolmarm's face. "Any new books in the library this week?"

"What did you two talk about over coffee?" Hamish asked Campbell.

"Nothing much," Campbell said. "Life."

"*Life?*"

"Yeah. Like I said. Nothing much, only – life." He said, imitating Hamish's voice. "Right?" he asked Théophile.

Théophile winked at me, but strangely; I turned to Campbell with puzzlement, and his eyes narrowed with a curious depth of feeling.

"That is true," Théophile said. "We spoke only of life."

Hamish, Nicolas, Campbell and I came up the stairs from the Concorde métro station and crossed with the light on rue de Rivoli, found our way to the bookstore, were directed upstairs, and made our way to our reserved seats in the front row. I found myself sitting between India, who for some reason immediately clutched Campbell's right arm, and Théophile's mother.

"You're almost late," India said to us.

Théophile's mother smiled at Campbell and then made a face at my shoes.

"They're Mephisto," I hissed.

She made an innocent-me-shrug and said to India, "*Mais quelle est la couleur ? Comment s'appelle-t-elle ?*"

"Beige," Nicolas said seriously, from where he sat on her other side. "The colour is beige. I like it and I like the shoes, they are stylish."

"Thanks," I said, in surprise and gratitude. I liked having Nicolas defend me; after all, you had to be of Nicolas's social level to stand up to Madame Legrêle-Chevrier.

"I didn't see you over there, my dear," India told Nicolas, having heard his comment about my shoes. "You're the one Marigold thinks is longing after Hamish."

"I am Nicolas," he said, his cheeks flushed, "And I do regard Hamish highly, but I assure you that I am not longing after him."

"*Mom*," Campbell said.

"Oh, hush. Nice shirt," she told me. "The colour suits you."

"Thanks. This is Théophile's mother," I said under my breath to Campbell. "Please ignore her."

"If you wonder why I'm holding on to Campbell like this," India said, "it's because he's been flexing his muscle for me. It's quite something. I can't see how pumped up biceps are helpful in modelling evening wear, but I suppose it pays to be versatile. Evening wear one day, internet porn as necessary to top up your bank account – just tweet your fans and update your status, I imagine it's all very modern these days, Polish porn, internet sites, modelling and –" She released Campbell's arm and patted his leg.

"You good?" Campbell asked, shaking his head at his mother's silliness.

"Great," I said, then to Hamish, who sat on the far side of Campbell. "Hi."

"Hi."

Balfour walked up to the podium, adjusted his glasses, and opened a book. He wore a burgundy smoking jacket, a cream-colored cravat, a pair of chinos and tasselled loafers. He shifted his glasses toward the end of his nose. "Before I start," he said, moving so that he looked directly at Hamish, "I'd like to acknowledge my son Hamish, who lives here in Paris. Hamish, thank you."

I turned and saw Hamish brighten up; he actually smiled at his father. Wonders will never cease, I thought, as a smattering of applause rippled around the room.

Balfour had finished and applause reverberated around the room. By dint of public pressure, everyone stood. I generally viewed standing ovations as awkward.

"I'm not staying for the signing," I told Campbell. "I need to get Miss Thing here into a taxi."

"I'll come with you," he said, trying to signal to Hamish but finding it impossible.

Hamish had been besieged by Balfour Bedminster groupies – and Javier, who had mysteriously appeared, had his strong arm over Hamish's shoulder protecting him. They made a striking couple. India had been embraced by a woman in rippling red organza, who spoke to her in an Italian accent. Marigold and Nicolas had gone up to the podium, the first in line to congratulate Balfour.

"I can't seem to say goodbye to anyone," Campbell said. "And where did Javier come from? That's him isn't it? Jesus, he's gorgeous."

"Yes – and yes – and he must have been lurking in the shadows. He's something of a minor television celebrity, so I'm sure he has his ways."

We looked around us at the chaos.

"I know," I said, "these events are always messy in France. What they can do with animal organs defies belief, but for some reason, even under a State of Emergency, they can't do crowd control."

I offered my arm to Théophile's mother and walked her through the crowd. Her imperious demeanour cleared a path for us.

"*J'aimerais parler avec Monsieur Balfour*," she said.

"*Pas possible, Maman.* She wants to speak with Balfour," I told Campbell. "But I've nixed that."

"*Mais le livre – sa signature ?*"

"*Je vous l'apporte plus tard.*" I turned to Campbell. "Honestly, I deserve combat pay for this." We made our way down the stairs and out to the Rue de Rivoli. On the street, we were jostled by throngs of people and Campbell offered his body as a barrier for Théophile's mother – who seemed charmingly misplaced there, a remnant of another age.

"Was there ever a time when Paris wasn't overrun with tourists?" I asked.

"I wouldn't know," Campbell said.

"What are they all here for? It isn't cheap, God knows. What are they hoping to see?"

"Paris," Campbell said simply.

I watched a bedraggled family fight the crowds, then he snorted derisively. "Wouldn't they be better off at an amusement park somewhere?"

"Possibly," Campbell agreed. "Better value for money, that's for sure."

With Théophile's mother now clinging to him, Campbell pushed our way through the crowd. As soon as we reached the street, she held one elegant hand out and a taxi glided to a stop in front of them.

"Nice work, *Maman*."

"*Merci*," she said, but it was unclear whether she spoke to me or to Campbell, who had opened the back door for her.

"*Je vous en prie*," Campbell said, startling me.

It prompted an almost beatific look from Théophile's mother, as she settled into the seat. "You are a nice man," she said in clear, crisp English. The door slammed shut and the taxi scooted off into the river of traffic on the Rue de Rivoli.

"That's the perfect thing to say to a woman her age," I told him.

"I'll try to remember that."

"Are you being sarcastic at my expense, oh former lover?"

"Caught that did you?"

"I wonder how much English she really does know?" I asked.

"Enough to keep score, I'd say."

I shrugged at that and we turned away from the kerb. As we did so, we were struck by a leathery, nearly nude man on inline skates – he knocked Campbell's shoulder square on and scraped my arm. In the aftermath, we found ourselves in one another's arms, steadying one other. But the moment lingered and ignited an erotic flame. I caressed Campbell's erection and then our lips met and held too long for the sidewalk.

Campbell pulled away first. "Whoa – okay – wow."

"Yes," I said, gasping, hands on Campbell's chest. "*Whoa – okay – wow*."

5

I climbed out a dormer window on the top floor landing, one of our building's nicer architectural flukes. Perched there on the roof, I leaned back against warm masonry. I had a keen need for isolation. Looking off toward the distant jumble of the Pantheon, I wondered if aristocratic wealth allowed Théophile to ignore Hamish's celebrity family. Celebrity did not impress Théophile; beauty and wit impressed Théophile. I coasted toward remembering the day we spread Didier and Benoît's ashes in Fontainebleau Forest. Prior to their deaths, I had never thought about dying, at least not seriously. Since that day, I thought of little else – though Campbell seemed suddenly to have returned sex to the list. I thought about Didier and Benoît, their eyes and arms and smells and smiles, the sound of their voices, those years of friendship. Would my own death come as it had for them, brutally disembowelled? Unexpectedly? Accidentally or purposely? Closing my eyes, I again pondered the fact that I would never again see my friends. My heart thumped with anxiety.

A besotted English boyfriend once gave me an ancient black and white photograph of a cricket game at Shrewsbury School in Shropshire. I loved it. A line of sweat visibly beaded a boy's forehead; sleeves rolled up, white pants stained with grass. Playing fields fell toward the river. The players rocked in the heavy air, wearied by heat, faces glistened, hair sagged. I always imagined glasses clinking in the pavilion, adult conversation buzzing beneath oak trees, punnets of cherries overflowing on blankets. The photographer captured it perfectly: players drifting toward the pavilion or along the grassy backs, arm-in-arm, summer happy. Cricket bats forsaken as fleecy clouds floated overhead. I always imagined forehead boy – as I dubbed him – and his best friend (he had to have one) flopping on their backs beneath a tree, the Severn River bubbling somewhere below them, the heat smothering, cricket whites dazzling against green grass. Their hands nearly held. They lay side by side. Vigorous young men, good-looking, all shoulders and long legs, blond and black hair, blue and brown eyes, promise and possibility, the friend with a flaxen aspect and a slight frame, and the other, a larger, more muscular body.

I thought at first that it was raining, but when I looked up at the sky, I realized the raindrops were my tears. Lifting my shirt, I lowered my face and dabbed my eyes.

"Campbell," I whispered, "*would* you have married me?"

Of course, there was no answer, just the rooftop rumble of a big city. I could not see Fontainebleau Forest from up there, though I wished to.

Turning on the bedroom light, I saw Théophile's suit tossed across the fauteuil in the corner. He had been home, changed, and then gone out to dinner? Plausible, but not Théophile's style. I went to his wardrobe and opened the door, searching for some clue. Probably off on a booze-up with his work chums in one of those disgusting nouveaux riches bars they favoured out in La Defense. I kicked off my shoes – perfectly appropriate for an afternoon reading, thank you very much, and hadn't Nicolas said as much? – and walked down to the kitchen. I poured myself a glass of wine and stood a moment at the kitchen window, looking into the courtyard of the neighbouring synagogue. The kiss with Campbell had rattled me. There was something so old school about an unforeseen kiss on the pavement – too romantic, like the *Umbrellas of Cherbourg* or *Ryan's Daughter.*

I drank the glass of wine and poured another. Oh, for God's sake, a kiss is just a kiss, wasn't that the song from *Casablanca*? I took my new glass of wine into the living room and flopped on the sofa. I should have changed my clothes, but I was too lazy now. Hamish would shriek when I told him about the kiss. Of course, I would tell him. I had actually wanted to tell him even as it happened. You had a best friend in order to share such things as unforeseen kisses on the rue de Rivoli, although my best friendship with Hamish seemed increasingly to be on autopilot – or perhaps a death spiral. Uncurling my legs, I got up and went to the *portes-fenêtres*, where I looked across the courtyard. Neighbours got ready for bed, watched television, worked on computers. Soon, they would all be staring over here, watching my thirtieth birthday party – or what they could see of it. They would hear more than they saw. How many would complain? I would send Campbell to deal with them. The thought of him confronting the elderly upstairs neighbours made me smile. They were used to the honeyed tones of Théophile's genteel French.

My clothes irritated me now, so I stripped down to my boxers and let my expensive shirt and chinos fall in a pool on the floor. I preferred posing at the *portes-fenêtres* in my underwear or, rather, the image of myself posing there. It seemed a more appropriate pose for someone who had been kissed – or who had kissed – on the rue de Rivoli. I wished my CRS boys could see me like this. I finished the class of wine and put it on the floor. Don't overreact, I repeated to myself like a mantra, let the pheromones settle. In the first hours after such an event, you were bound to be all lathered up. I stretched, left the windows, and went to the mantle – stuffed with years-long collections of Little Prince knick-knacks, all of them gifts from Hamish.

I touched the three pen-and-pencil sets with their maudlin quotations, like *il faut chercher avec le cœur*. That one, in particular, struck me as inane. You have to search with your heart. What bullshit. I knocked on the heads of several of the Little Prince dolls in their different costumes – pilot, scholar, man on safari – and all seven of the paperweights. When I reached the blue and gold thermometer, I lingered, running my index finger up and down the indicator. "What a bunch of crap," I said, not posing now, not imagining a tableau. I picked up the thermometer and two of the dolls, which was all I could carry, and stepped back to the window. I leaned forward and dropped them. Thunks and smashes echoed around the courtyard. I stood there listening to the dying echoes. Then, I turned off the lights and went to shower. How fortunate that Théophile had chosen tonight – although it was Friday, after all – for his work chums booze-up. I could shower, lounge in bed with a book, take a Temazapam (or two) and then drift off to sleep. I flicked off the hallway lights.

I stood in the bedroom behind the sheer curtains, watching Théophile on the phone in the living room. The L-shape of the apartment made it possible to peer across the courtyard from one room to another. I hadn't woken up when Théophile came in last night, so I had no idea what time it had been – and yet I'd slept longer and felt groggy and Théophile chirped away on the phone. Théophile rarely used the phone on the weekends, except for business, and business rarely made him smile. He seemed curiously animated this morning, standing shirtless in a pair of his Saturday jeans at the living room *portes-fenêtres*. I saw him guffaw – *truly uncharacteristic* – then he turned away from the window and disappeared. I found an old shirt to wear and walked down the hall to where he now stood in the kitchen fixing coffee. He no longer talked on the phone.

"What's your story?" I asked.

"Short or long version, English or French?"

"Oh, good grief. Are you still drunk? You're never such a jolly chipmunk on Saturday morning."

"Of course, I am," he said, without turning around from the coffee maker.

"No, you're not." I looked out the window at the neighbouring synagogue. "What time did you get in last night?"

"I've no idea."

"Of course, you do. You fucking know what time you tie your shoes and the hourly conversion rate for the Hong Kong Dollar."

He clicked the coffee cone shut and turned the machine on. "Why do you need to know what time I came home?"

I looked at him. "I don't need to know; I want to know."

"About three," He said. "And I'm not drunk."

The coffee started gurgling and the pot began to fill with its fragrant sludge. "How's your testosterone work gang?"

"My what?"

"Those La Défense wheelers and dealers with whom you work."

"My co-workers are the same as always, I presume. Why are you asking after them?"

"Because presumably you were out with them last night."

"No," He said. "I wasn't out with them."

"You don't have to lie. I'm not a fool."

"Why do people say that? Everyone is a fool in some way."

"This is what comes from studying philosophy for your BAC," I said, watching the pot fill with coffee. "Frenchmen are all philosophers. I am – of course, you're right, foolish in many ways, known and unknown. I simply meant that I had figured out what you were up to last night."

"You figured out that I was with my co-workers?"

"Along with a few boozy bimbos and Rugby argot."

He glanced down at the coffee and laughed.

"What's so funny?"

"Nothing is funny; absolutely nothing in our lives is funny, Justin."

"But you're laughing."

"You're making many observations this morning." He stretched, holding his arms up over his head. "I was at a dinner party with my parents. I did not invite you because I knew you would not come. Besides, my mother is displeased with you."

"By way of a change."

"Nothing to do with your clothes, however."

"Trust me, she has an opinion on my clothes. And?"

"And what, Justin?

"And what the fuck is the matter with you?"

"Many things are the matter with me, the fuck and other-wise. But none of them are small enough to be discussed in the kitchen on a Saturday morning. Perhaps after your birthday."

"*Huh?*"

"What is the matter with me demands at least an entire Tuesday evening to unravel. But, as you say, this is what comes from studying philosophy for the BAC."

"What's that noise?" I asked, looking again out the window at the synagogue, ignoring Théophile's Tuesday evening announcement. The synagogue occasionally turned noisy on Saturdays.

"Buses."

"*Buses?*"

"They've diverted buses down our street."

"Oh, shit. Perfect. Buses chundering down the street on Saturday."

"Must be something going on today, perhaps involving your CRS boys, no doubt speaking police argot about boozy bimbos."

"My CRS boys?" I said, but with an embarrassingly tell-tale blush.

He shrugged and smiled. "One has his sources, *chéri.*"

He poured us both cups of coffee. I took the coffee from his hand. "What large – whatever it was you said?" Justin asked.

"After your birthday, *chéri.* We have a plan."

I looked at him and thought of my favourite line from *Breakfast at Tiffany's* (which had once been my bible, before I discovered Victoria Carlyle and *Sense and Sensibility*), 'No matter where you run, you just end up running into yourself.'

Marigold and I walked in the direction of Luxembourg Garden, from the Carrefour de l'Odeon. When we reached the Marché St. Germain, the part of our neighbourhood I disliked, we turned right in order to walk around the shopping mall. I felt crabby just strolling between the modern edifice of the shopping mall – with its snappy-snazzy Apple store (where they were unbearably rude, even by European standards) – and the pre-Second Empire dwarf apartments across the street, toad remnants of a Paris that had not yet mastered rudimentary capitalism, let alone international electronics franchises. Of course, the neighbourhood was made worse by the proliferation of my two least favourite groups: illegal migrants, who were fed daily on the far side of the mall, and tourists, who infested the mall as if they had discovered – *at last* – a Paris that made sense to them.

"I hate this part of the quartier," I muttered.

Marigold looked around; it clearly didn't seem hateable to her.

"*T'es un voleur*," I said, glowering at a migrant with a dirty red scarf on his head, pushing a shopping cart.

"You told him he was a thief?" Marigold asked in surprise, watching as the man and his shopping cart scuttled off into the shadows behind the mall's faux colonnades.

"He is. *What?* Like Marks & Spencers gives their shopping carts away?"

We crossed over rue Saint Sulpice and walked beside St. Sulpice Church, from where we walked up the narrow, cobbled length of rue Ferou, crossed through the traffic on Rue Vaugirard, and approached the park entrance by the *Orangerie*. A mêlée spread over the pavement, where a crowd attempted to squish through the gates. Senate guards in black-billed caps – supposedly there to maintain order – engaged in cheerful badinage with a woman in a leather mini-skirt. Soldiers with long guns scanned the crowds for suicide bombers. Holding my elbow out like a hammer, I sluiced through the crowd with ruthless efficiency: either that or a panic attack. I led us to my favourite bench, where once upon a time I had sat intimately with Théophile.

"When he's in Paris, Campbell always goes running in Luxembourg gardens," Marigold said.

"It's a thing to do. Campbell always does the things you do if you're trying to be hip."

"Which he is."

"Yes," I agreed. "Though occasionally over the top. Do you remember when he had that ridiculous poem published."

"Back when poetry was hip?"

"*Touché.*" I said.

"And it wasn't ridiculous at all, Justin, it was sensitive and beautiful: 'There is no secret, and that's the puzzle. Because we desire mystery and fear of something unknown. We search for the key to a box unlocked, wishing it sealed, so like Pandora, we might unleash some, fast fiery fury, to hurry our world, and let loose our hounds of desire and love.'"

"No," I said, stunned by her recollection of the poem, as well as the intensity of the imagery. Campbell had always played at being a bubblehead; that's what made him both romantically inaccessible as well as occasionally dangerous, "It's not ridiculous. But come to think of it, when *was* poetry hip?"

"The 1800s – the 1950s and 60s. Coleridge had his fair share of ridiculous over-the-toppers," Marigold said. "Though I love them."

"And I think Kipling had something that was one line – maybe two," I said.

"If any question why we died, tell them, because our fathers lied.' It's actually part of 'Epitaphs of the War,' and personally I prefer the part that comes right after: 'Now all my lies are proved untrue, and I must face the men I slew. What tale shall serve me here among, mine angry and defrauded young.'"

"Bloody Hell," I gasped. "I thought he was the great defender of Imperialism and all that."

"He was, until he lost his only son John in The Great War and then he more or less went off the deep end. His son was killed just a few weeks after his eighteenth birthday. Strangely, Mrs. Kipling more or less carried on – for the sake of the

neighbours, she apparently wrote in her diary, *of all idiocies* –
but Rudyard never came right. He was a total wreck."

"I identify with the wrecked Kipling," I said softly. "Fuck
Mrs. Kipling and the neighbours.

"I shouldn't have told you all of that. What was I thinking?"
She gave me that I-know-you're-wounded look to which I'd
grown accustomed.

We sat quietly and listened to the birds. The fountain
and its gravel circle spread out before us. I loved this view of
the garden and the fountain, which made me think of the
1920s: Hemingway, F. Scott Fitzgerald, Gertrude Stein and
Alice B. Toklas, Sylvia Beach, Josephine Baker, French children with nannies and sailboats. I went through long periods
during which I never came to the Luxembourg Garden, then
prompted by something – Marigold's offer, for instance, or
watching a television programme, in which the park featured
prominently – I'd come and be charmed again. When young
and in love with Paris I spent hours here, writing in jour-
nals, flirting, even occasionally sleeping in stippled sunlight
on benches. Théophile proposed to me on the sward of gravel
at the bottom of the park, where the *Observatoire* loomed. We
had come here for a walk and had been kissing. Inevitable, his
proposal, and not my fondest memory of the park. Having sex
with a wickedly handsome waiter named Christophe, would
always hold pride of place; his kisses made my toes curl, and
he screwed me in the October leaves like an animal. I felt
somewhat sentimental about that French waiter.

"However," I said, "I don't see Campbell as Kipling or
Coleridge."

Marigold merely shrugged. She lifted her sunglasses up to
her hair and touched my arm a moment. She noticed my hand.
"*Oh.* You've cut yourself."

I looked at the puckered wound. "On my window."

"What are you? A self-mutilator?"

"*Yup.*"

She smiled a beguiling Marigold smile, no doubt the same smile that once seduced Nethersole; I saw she that she chose to disbelieve me.

"Isn't it beautiful?" Marigold asked, looking out over the fountain.

"Yes."

"It must all have been such a nightmare, Justin" she said.

"You're not imagining I'll disagree, are you?"

"No, of course not. I live in Australia, I rarely watch the news and I almost never read a paper but even I felt upended by it. One hundred and thirty lives lost, most of them young, *in one night*, and so soon after Charlie Hebdo – and then with the eighty-four in Nice. My God, Justin."

"It was – actually, I don't know how to describe what it was. I only wish it were in the past tense, but it isn't. Every day I wake up and I think of Didier and Benoît and how they died. How can you die like that? They were nice guys, you know? Didier, I'd even call him innocent. He volunteered, he gave money to causes, and then –," I choked up, paused, collected myself. "I want to move on, but I can't. Dr. Beaunier and my pharmacy of drugs keep me *almost* sane, but not moving on. I'm like Kipling, forever done in by my bereavement."

Marigold's eyes brimmed with tears and she took both of my hands in her own; she said nothing; nothing to say, really.

I pointed. "See those trees through there? By the corner? Some guy tried to fuck me standing up – third tree in."

"*Tried?*"

"He had a weak back or something, though to look at it – which I did while he was playing tennis *sans chemise* – you'd have thought it was plenty strong. Tried to fuck me is being generous. I think they heard my screams of pain in Lithuania. How's Gareth's back, by the way?"

"Plenty strong. To look at it, at any rate." She released my hands and looked off across the fountain. "You and Hamish have been best friends for a long time."

"Twelve years," I said.

"That's a long time."

"Yes," I agreed. Coming from Marigold's mouth it astonished me. I sat upright. "It is."

India, Balfour, Marigold, Campbell, Hamish, Nicolas, and I had spread ourselves drunkenly around Nicolas's living room. We had already ploughed through several bottles of Champagne. Shirt off, wearing a pair of jeans, Campbell sprawled over one end of the sofa; In desperate need of reassurance, I stretched out on the floor beneath his feet, while Marigold sat with her legs curled up on the other end; India sat in one of the *fauteuils* and Balfour in another. Nicolas had collapsed in another plush chair, long legs stretched in front of him. Hamish sat on the floor next to Balfour's chair, his head leaning from time to time against the puffy arm.

"You've had enough champagne for one night," Balfour said to India, who had just finished a ribald joke.

"Hush. I'm ignoring you, Mr. Magoo," she said, waving dismissively at him.

"Why are you calling him Mr. Magoo?" Hamish asked.

"Because he's myopic; he can't see what's going on right in front of him."

"Like most writers," Balfour said, "I'm profoundly unobservant."

"No need for hyperbole, Magoo, unobservant speaks for itself."

"Who is this Mister Magoo?" Nicolas wondered.

"Some ancient American cartoon character," Marigold said, "who was near-sighted and bumbling,"

"Sound familiar?" India asked.

"TV Guide ranked Mr. Magoo number twenty-nine on its 'Fifty Greatest Cartoon Characters of All Time' list," Balfour said.

"Always the source to which *I* turn," India sniffed.

"Is there something going on between you two?" Hamish asked.

"Sadly, not much has gone on between the two of us for ten years, darling. I'm planning on at least one more glass of this superb champagne, in case you think you have any influence over my drinking," she said to Balfour.

"You're being outrageous tonight, mom," Hamish said. "That usually means you're upset."

"And you only fight with dad when something's bothering you," Marigold added.

"Otherwise," Balfour said, "she ignores me. I'm not sure which I prefer."

"*Upset?* God forbid I should be upset," India said. "Just look at the state of the world. An ageing, bloated, insecure buffoon with his tiny fingers on the nuclear arsenal? It's hardly something to laugh about, is it?" She twisted her necklace for a moment. "Though I have laughed at dark moments, it's true. Do you remember when Lady Cynthia whatever-her-name was, gave that fake eulogy at mother's funeral? And she was waving around that little crow hand of hers and her ring kept clinking against the urn with mother's ashes? I'd never seen anything so ludicrous as that idiot prattling on about how nice mother was – enough to laugh at right there – and mother clinking in disagreement from out of her urn."

"More champagne?" Campbell offered, holding up the bottle.

"Don't mind if I do, young man." India held her glass out and he filled it.

Everyone else declined, so Campbell downed some directly from the bottle. "Good stuff," he said with a small burp.

I looked around at these lovely, irreverent people gathered in a beautiful space. Nicolas seemed especially handsome tonight, stretched out in his chair, sleeves rolled up, arm veins exposed in masculine insouciance, hair mussed, eyes gleaming, champagne glass held at a jaunty angle.

Taking a sip of her champagne, India said, "A toast to our almost-birthday boy. Justin, you have lived life fully, even if you are often insufferable and self-indulgent." Another sip of champagne. "Some people are objects by choice. Justin, I admire your decision to be one of them. Ah, my lad, you've put many footprints on many ceilings."

It took a moment for the comment to register.

"God, mom," Campbell said. "That's like so harsh."

"You're half untucked, lovey," India said to Nicolas, whose shirt had nearly come out from his trousers. Justin thought he looked like someone who had awakened from a sweaty nap, his shirt wrinkled and loose. "And it's not harsh – it's true."

"Being true doesn't make it unharsh." Campbell's colour had come up, with bright red splotches on his cheeks.

"Unharsh is not a word," India said. "And Justin, like you, is a physical being – a sex loving demi-heathen."

"A *what?*" I said.

"Please. You have had a lot of joy out of being fucked – often – and with a variety of fuckers. You're straight from the pages of D. H. Lawrence, except for the gay part, he was a tad repressed about his sexuality, wasn't he?"

Campbell and his mother stared at one another; Nicolas looked at me, with a wide-eyed sort of protective – something.

"You get much out of life, our Justin, which is what I thought we had decided to celebrate this evening." She raised her champagne glass. "So, to Justin and his gusto for life, and to how he never forgets what he wants and when he wants it."

"You can be a cold-hearted bitch, mother."

India seemed taken with that. She even smiled. "Really? Then I was right when I told Marigold that Justin had become like a son to me." She closed her eyes a moment, then opened them, glistening with tears.

Campbell finished off his bottle of champagne. His lower lip pouted, he ran a hand petulantly through his hair. India took a deep breath, leaned her head back, and closed her eyes again. For some reason, I felt untroubled by her purposefully mean remarks (and by all rights *I* should have been furious). Instead, I saw her as vulnerable and ageing, which I had never done before; she had become a new India Chatterton, and one that I liked much less. Nicolas stared at me empathetically; Campbell pouted like a hairy-chested James Dean.

"Favourite song," Hamish said. "Everyone's favourite song."

"We're playing party games now?" India asked.

"It's one of Justin's things."

"Oh, Hell," I said. "That was aeons ago. But you're right. I thought it was cool. I remember making everyone do it at some, *what?* Clambake or something – you know, Campbell, that summer."

"Yes, dear," India said, "we all know – *that summer.*"

"'Wild Thing,' by the Troggs," Balfour said, then he burst out laughing. "I love this song. It's even on my phone."

"Nice, dad," Campbell said, his pouting over, appreciatively scratching his stomach and then bringing his hand to rest on his Pecs, seeming to have forgotten – or forgiven – India's remarks. Only Nicolas seemed to have a simmering resentment, hidden behind his French gentility; I saw it bubbling in his bold blue eyes.

"Wild thing, I think you move me," Balfour said, closing his eyes to concentrate. "But I gotta know for sure. Come on and hold me tight. Oh, you move me –" and he roared once again with laughter.

"Who is this man?" India said, sipping her champagne, and pointing at Balfour with the toe of one high heel. "I trust you're laughing with shame."

Then she warbled, "I am the Very Model of a Modern Major General," paused to sip more champagne, "Gilbert and Sullivan." She peered at them over the top of her glass. "How do you like them apples?"

"What the Hell's that?" Campbell asked. "I've never even heard of it."

"Which eliminates nine tenths of western culture," India said.

"That can't possibly be your favourite," Marigold said in shock, spluttering a bit of her champagne.

"Good grief, mom," Hamish said, "Get real. It's not even a song song, it's a –"

"But it is," I said, clapping my hands, "And I adore it."

Then out of the blue, "I'm very good at integral and differential calculus," Nicolas sang, his voice a rich baritone, "I know the scientific names of beings animalculous; In short, in matters vegetable, animal, and mineral, I am the very model of a modern Major-General." Everyone sat in silence; stunned. "From one of my English classes at the Sorbonne – to improve our diction. We had some other choices, of course, but that was mine. I even wore a big hat when I sang it."

"What kind of hat?" Marigold asked.

"Something English, I don't remember – I got it at a costume shop in Montmartre. I think it was Lord Nelson's hat, but it suited well enough when I was singing."

Had I known that Nicolas went to the Sorbonne? If so, I'd forgotten.

"Shit," Campbell whistled. "You are the dude, Nicolas. That's so totally cool." And then he announced, "'I Love New York,' Madonna," and he stood up. Using his champagne glass as a microphone, he sang, "Other cities always make me mad, other places always make me sad. No other city ever made me glad except New York. I love New York. If you don't like my attitude then you can F- off. Just go to Texas, isn't that where they golf? New York is not for little pussies who scream. If you can't stand the heat, then get off my street."

Everyone clapped; Campbell bowed.

"My beautiful nudist porn star singer son," India said.

"Why are your clothes always off, if I might ask?" Balfour said, in a surprisingly serious voice, considering the frivolous circumstances.

"Because I love the way my body looks." Campbell shrugged dismissively. "And I love the effect it has on other people. I totally love watching people get turned on by me."

"And which of us here, pray tell, would be the target audience for getting turned on?" India said, looking rather too obviously at me. "Or maybe you're just going for a general admiration effect?"

Watching Campbell's face, catching his glance, I realized that what Campbell almost said – what he wanted to say – was, 'Justin.' For another moment, his eyes met mine and I knew he flirted with me; but, of course, it might just have been because I'd always been hot-to-trot whenever Campbell took off his shirt. He smiled his I'm-being-patient-with-Mom smile and said, "A cool body is a cool body, Mom. Admit it: you can't take your eyes off me."

"Like when I visit the zoo."

"Whatever." Campbell waved his hand across the room at Nicolas.

"Do it, Nicolas. Take it off. Show them. Be cool, dude. Let them love your body."

To everyone's surprise – but most especially to mine, since I had created an image of Nicolas that in no way included a drunken Chippendale's routine – he put down his champagne glass, unbuttoned his shirt, took it off, and tossed it on the floor. Standing up, he proceeded to turn slowly around like a model, until he had come back to face us with a smile. "I love my body too," he said.

"How about that?" Campbell asked, his voice like a proud father. He turned to me. "Look at him. You're magnificent, dude."

"Thank you," Nicolas said.

Nicolas had transmogrified – as Campbell suggested – into someone other than the character we had created for our quotidian booze-ups; I struggled to reconfigure his place in our world, this man with a deliciously hairy chest who looked like a centrefold, and in no way resembled the after-work dishevelled Nicolas of an evening at the Café.

Since he had our attention, Nicolas announced, "'Surfin' Safari,' the Beach Boys," and then he did a version of a dance that resembled the twist while singing, "If ev'rybody had an ocean across the U.S.A., then ev'rybody'd be surfin' like Californ-I-A. You'd see 'em wearin' their baggies. Huarachi sandals, too. A bushy, bushy blonde hairdo. Surfin' U.S.A."

"And you have the hairdo," Hamish said, smiling.

Nicolas fell back in his chair, laughing.

India finished her animated clapping, gawking almost greedily at Nicolas – flopped there picturesquely, laughing as much to himself as with his audience. Then she turned to Hamish, and pointing a finger at him, said sternly, "Get a clue, sunshine – before it's too late."

"Before what's too late?" Hamish asked.

"Don't be dense. I tolerated you being dense when you were in high school, because you had so much to be embarrassed about – sports humiliations and wanting to take home economics and making that wedding dress for Marigold's Barbie doll out of tissues. Surely you remember *that* escapade, Marigold?"

Marigold shrugged a quick smile at Hamish, the smile of the mother of five children, understanding and accepting.

"Little Marigold took it around to show all of the shocked Republican neighbours? Am I right?"

"I think Eleonor Farnsworth across the street was the only one shocked," Marigold said.

"That was sufficient – the woman lived to gossip." India gulped back the rest of her champagne. "But I'm tolerating denseness no longer."

"And you are famed for your tolerance, mother," Marigold said with a yawn.

"I am famed for many things, fortunately and *unfortunately*, truthfully and untruthfully."

Of course, I knew that India enjoyed being shocking. But something seemed distinctly off with her tonight – but not just tonight. Something hurt in her. Could it simply be her artistic quandary?

Marigold stood up, "I won't go into the details of the way Justin once managed to twist my adoration of our beloved Australian national icon Kylie Minogue into something lurid."

"Oh, but please do," India said. "I have a penchant for unrequited lesbian love stories."

"Since when?" Campbell asked.

"Since the age of fourteen, when my Great Aunt Mary told me about her mad passion for Djuna Barnes, when she lived in Paris in the 1930s. So there."

"June-ah *who?*"

"Hush," Marigold told them, "Suffice it to say that Justin agreed with me that this song, which I sent to him as an Mp3, is utterly brilliant." A bit off key at first, but then with gathering poise, she gave a straight-backed rendition of a verse of "I Believe in You": "I don't believe that beauty will ever be replaced; I don't believe a masterpiece could ever match your face; The joker's always smiling in every hand that's dealt; I don't believe that when you die your presence isn't felt."

After a moment of astonished absorption of the words, we all clapped vigorously and with a mock bow she sat back down on her chaise. "Justin," Marigold said. "I do believe you're up next."

"True," Hamish agreed.

I dutifully stood up and watched their faces as I sang, "Ah, ooh, Werewolves of London, You can hear him howling around your kitchen door, Better not let him in, Little old lady got mutilated late last night, Werewolves of London again, Ah, ooh, Werewolves of London, He's the hairy-handed gent that ran amuck in Kent, Lately he's been overheard in Mayfair."

A longish silence lasted until Javier and Théophile surprised us all by appearing in the doorway.

"I have come to collect my wayward boyfriend, from what appears to be a strip-tease at the Crazy Horse," Javier said.

"Quite right," Balfour said, going over so that he could shake their hands. "They've been throwing their shirts off like professionals in Las Vegas. Though fully clad, Justin has just treated us to a werewolf tune."

"Yes," Théophile said, coming over and putting a hand on my shoulder. "I heard."

India stood up, saying, "Wasn't all that special? Come along, Balfour. Take me back to that hotel you claim to love. And you, young man," she said to Nicolas with a wink, reaching over and ruffling his hair with enthusiastic affection, "are the best thing since sliced bread."

6

As I came off the elevator after work I found Javier sitting on the landing in front of our door.

"What are you doing out here in the dark?" I gasped.

Of course, the stairwell light came on when the elevator door opened; nonetheless, he had possibly been sitting in the dark for a long time. Given his appearance of sweaty discomfort, he must have been. Perspiration circles spread under the arms of his shirt. Always hot in the stairwell during the summer, no matter how many landing windows the Gardien opened – but that offered even greater reason *not* to sit there, with or without lights.

"I've been waiting for you," he said.

We looked at one another.

"You could have called me." I held out my phone for emphasis. "Did you get the digi-codes from Hamish?"

"I found them – in his wallet."

"Ah. *Okay.*"

We exchanged a look that felt too intense.

"I think you need to take a break from Hamish."

"This is some kind of Reverse Cyrano de Bergerac? You're breaking up with me on behalf of Hamish?"

"You are a destructive influence."

"Says you or says Hamish?" I asked, flustered, my anxiety rising now.

Javier merely stared at me.

Halted in mid-motion, I stared back. All kinds of things came to mind to say, yet nothing felt right. After all, once someone tells you that you are a destructive influence, it's beyond the talking stage, isn't it? If Javier had wanted to talk, he would not have said things so resolutely; he would have left a door open. Lost somewhere in an emotional triangle of despair, anger and panic, I continued to stare at him; he returned the favour. A door opened and slammed somewhere in the building; someone's footsteps echoed down the stairwell. The buzzer sounded, the front door opened and closed. Still we stared at one another.

"Come in?" I managed at last to say.

"No."

"I love Hamish. He's my best friend."

"No, you do not love him. In fact, you look embarrassed when you say it. Frankly, it's a friendship of convenience that holds Hamish a prisoner to your sarcastic whims."

I felt myself flush. I could again think of nothing to say.

Javier stood up. "I put your keys into the mailbox in the lobby. I'm certain Hamish will be angry at first when I tell him, but he now has no way to come into your apartment. It's best. I've already changed the locks on Hamish's apartment, so you can throw your set of keys away."

Then quickly he walked down the stairs, brushing past me.

I inhaled an intoxicating final whiff of his Javier smell of soap, perspiration and potting soil. My eyes welled up with tears. When I turned around, I could not even see him on the stairs, though I could hear his running footsteps descend to the lobby.

"Goodbye," I said, far too quietly to be heard of course, and whether I said it to Javier or Hamish I couldn't have said. The front door buzzed open and fell shut with a bang.

The light, still operating off its timer, plinked off and the stairwell plunged into darkness.

"Goodbye," I said again.

I lay in bed pondering a mysterious early-morning text from India, summoning me to a meeting. Throwing off the duvet, I sat up and shifted to the edge of the bed. I still felt too angry with Javier to think clearly, and the amount of diazepam I took last night would have dropped a moose. How dare he? I stood up and went to the wardrobe, where I saw my fingers tremble on the handle with wrath. Of course, I had been angry with Javier for a long time – he had never fit into our group. Now, opening the door and plucking my robe off its hanger, I thought I had been a colossal wimp during our exchange in the stairwell. I'd allowed him to treat me disrespectfully. As I went into the kitchen and began making coffee, the idea came to me and I felt the wind shift. Going into the living room, I picked up my phone. I began practicing my lines, going through different scenarios – stingingly strong or low-key words with venom behind them. What worked best with someone like Javier? Phone in hand, I stepped to the window and watched some doves in the courtyard.

I stood there, feet on the sill, arms braced against the frame. The breeze ruffled up beneath my robe; it fluttered magically, warm wind tickling my nakedness. I stood in the window for at least ten minutes, trying to summon the nerve to jump. Several times I let go of the frame and nearly – *nearly* – did it. But at the last minute I grasped the frame and stood there forlorn in the breeze. It should be easy to jump, I thought:

flutter, ruffle, and a thump as I hit the courtyard. People would hear the thump and come running, so I needed to think about how I landed – face up would be best, if I could contrive it. I had seen this on an episode of a television programme, and even though the man broke every bone in his body, his face remained untouched, still handsome, rather like the apocryphal stories one heard about the death of Princess Diana.

Of course, I might end up a paraplegic or a brain damaged creature with a walker. The fall came with no guarantee of death. This fall didn't come close to the television programme guy's leap off a London skyscraper. I leaned further out and the breeze teased my hair. I closed my eyes. When I opened them, I found myself looking across the courtyard into the apartment India had admired; it glowed with colour. 'Two years ago,' I thought, 'I owned this city and every goddamned gay man in it.' I stepped down from the window and turned back to the phone, having settled on iron hard anger – uncompromising, condemnatory, tough. I could do this: I could be strong. I concentrated. Then, summoning my will, I punched the numbers and felt my breath wedge somewhere in my chest – my heart hammering – sweat forming on my palms.

"*Bonjour,*" the voice said, "*C'est Javier. Laissez votre message après le bip sonore.*"

I disengaged the call and hurled the phone across the room. It crashed into the Dolce Espresso coffee maker. I sat down fast on the window seat – and burst into tears. Once the tears passed, I took another Clonazepam, which seemed more useful than jumping out the window.

Over the years, you just naturally took friends for granted. You grew a little distant, didn't update your notes about one another. Instinctive. Hamish remained Hamish: he conveniently lived in Paris, he had a scholarly air about him. I'd been contented with that image, because such an image demanded no research or updating. It had been shocking – or something even more cosmic than that – to discover these fault lines, and to hear myself called a destructive influence. I thought about India's remark about how I lived on a stage set. Since Didier and Benoît's death at the Bataclan, make-believe had filled out the necessary corners of my drugged-up life, and Paris *had* become a stage set; not real at all.

I turned away from the window and flopped backward across the sofa. Of course, I had made these realizations myself. Fucking rough, however, to see your life as merely a stage set, your dreams painted backdrops. Also, the family and friend thing crushed me – aloof Théophile, Javier severing my friendship with Hamish, my father ignoring me, and India, gaunt and behaving strangely. I sat upright, enjoying the way my stomach muscles tightened, as they did during sit-ups. Going to the gym paid off – clearly – and I felt relieved that I didn't lie crumpled in the courtyard. I went toward the bathroom to shower, but stopped in the doorway. It came to me in what Marigold would call an epiphany: Javier had the guts to say what others also thought. I had become an insidious influence in Hamish's life, long before my PTSD. I stood there, considering the many ways my tentacles had wrapped themselves around Hamish.

I thought about how I had moulded – or tried to mould – my friend. I had always been the dominant partner in our friendship. Like a string of black and white vignettes, I remembered those summers – including the one of glorious fucking with Campbell – when Hamish stood on the periphery, sometimes even mocked by us. Why we mocked him I could not recall. Perhaps nothing more than the fact that he made easy bait. Even then, I had my artful way of withholding affection in order to get it. I sat a moment on the closed toilet seat.

What could I do? Phone up my former best friend and say, "Javier's right, run, I'm a black widow and I'm eating you alive?" Actually, I liked the idea of that conversation; something Balfour-ish about it. Of course, I didn't need to tell Hamish about Javier's visit. Hamish being Hamish, he would already have figured out my bad influence and endured it. He probably long ago felt trapped, and long ago saw no way out. No doubt he saw Javier as his saviour.

I felt teary again, despite the drug, and nearly picked up the phone to call Marigold. But instead of crying or calling or leaping from windows, I leaned my head back and thought about sex. Once, Théophile had willingly nailed me nightly in performances worthy of porn. Too bad I didn't have a camera around for those times. Honestly, I made Théophile brilliant – coming two, no three times – getting him to scream like a banshee (what was a banshee, anyway?) and come in undulating waves of pleasure. Yeah, I thought, I'm good. Everyone has his specialties, and excellent fucking is mine. I felt less clear just then about what the others might be. I glanced down at my growing erection, admiring the determination of the little devil after all of the medication. Twenty-nine and nine-tenths trumped medication any day; I cradled it gently.

Then I heard someone masculine on the television (which I had left babbling in the other room) that caused me to stand up and go to the door. Pointing my erection at him I listened as a France 2 reporter interviewed a stunning head of police counter-intelligence. Now, *that* was one hot man. Jesus. Truly, I thought, I would like to be screwed to the nearest wall by that police officer. Watching the handsome policeman flirt with the camera, I started to masturbate. The policeman laughed huskily and I stroked faster, finishing the business with amazing rapidity and wiping myself up with a towel.

Done with my trains of morbid thought about Hamish, I turned on the shower and climbed in. I thought I might bring India some flowers, it felt very Henry James in Paris. However, I had never read a word of Henry James, and his novels had undercurrents of racism, didn't they? I had recently watched something on television. Or had it been Evelyn Waugh? Things change, even the so-called Anglo-Saxon classics. I knew that something serious troubled India; I knew that she struggled to maintain her strength – she betrayed weakness in her bossing of Balfour, her bizarre snap decisions, sizzling the air with the burnt ozone of her wit, it all seemed like amateur theatrics. I got out of the shower and decided not to blow-dry my hair for fear now of waking Théophile, with whom I did *not* want to talk.

Having fluffed up my hair with a towel, I took a break from spraying it with my cactus and bamboo blossom hair-spray to mist Théophile's elegant horn-rim glasses, which he had left on the bathroom counter. I imagined him like India's myopic Mr. Magoo, trying to peer through the slime. Maybe he would run into the wall or trip over the toilet. I giggled out loud at that and gave them another quick spray for insurance. Finished with my beautifications, I quietly dressed, and glided out to the hallway, where I made my way to the elevator, down to the courtyards, and out to the street. I stopped at the news-stand, where the owner's son looked at me with his sexy short beard and mysteriously dark eyes. The man's cheekbones were phenomenal. I should ask Campbell to give me the name and email address of his porn agent. Looking into the eyes of the news agent's son, I had the prescient realization – and didn't Didier and Benoit prove it? – that the future is an illusion.

I tried in vain to gather round a flock of angels; this sudden helplessness startled me. Where had they gone? By then I had entered ZeroZero, the restaurant on the corner of Rue Vaneau and Rue de Sevres, and saw India look up from where she sat at a table in the farthest nook. Her face looked haggard; a face I had never seen on her. I moved toward her table, even as I still sent out silent, futile requests for angelic assistance. ZeroZero, one of India's places, always rolled out a genuine welcome. They seemed sincerely to like her. Perhaps she summoned me here today for that reason?

"Hello," she said, drying her eyes with the backs of her hands, as I sat down. She adjusted her suit, as if it were important not to look dishevelled, despite her tears.

"What's going on? You scared the life out of me this morning." I said.

"Is it your art crisis?"

"No," she said in a withering tone, "there is, in fact no art crisis. That was – is – subterfuge."

Her favourite server, Sindy, came over for bises and greetings, taking our orders for *Kir Royaux*, which I knew would arrive with an assortment of sausage slices, cherry tomatoes, and peanuts.

"Then – ?" I said, wounded by her remark, still nursing a vague ire over her comments about me at the song fest, and yet sensing that something had gone seriously wrong in her life. Impending divorce? Where the Hell had my angels gone?

Our Kirs arrived, along with small plates of dry sausage, tomatoes and peanuts, as I had predicted.

Wiping away fresh tears, India said, "Clearly you don't look me up on the internet, though I'm sure it's the first thing you'll do once we're through here."

I felt confused; of course, I had no reason to look up India. My psychiatrist did not encourage internet use, for good reasons.

India guzzled her Kir. "Speculation is rampant, and correct – for once."

I shook my head, lost in this morass of flummoxing emotion. India never expressed emotion, just words. *"India?"*

She finished her Kir and gestured to Sindy for another. Then she sighed and, looking out the window at an exceptionally handsome young man in the rain at the municipal bicycle rack, said, "Did you know I fired that worthless assistant of mine. She deserved to be fired, she was appalling. It was a fair dismissal, in fact it stood up in court despite her three lawsuits and four – I think – appeals. But she's mentally ill, sick, *sick*."

Sindy brought the second Kir and assessed our mood before leaving. I moved close enough to India for our arms to touch.

"Is that what's bothering you?" I asked.

"Nothing's bothering me," India said, "it's just that I'm dying, Justin. I have a glioblastoma, an inoperable brain tumour. It's a wretch of a thing, the bugger is shaped like a spiral and a pencil. I've decided against radiation, and the chemotherapy isn't likely to help at this stage. I endured the headaches for too long, I suppose, even though they had me screaming in pain all night long. I thought it was stress or Balfour or – Campbell's antics, I suppose."

She fell silent and looked at me. If she expected a response, then I disappointed her. I could think of nothing to say.

India sighed. "So I've been putting my affairs in order, I have perhaps another six to eight weeks before I'm stuck indoors. I'm already blurry eyed and wobbly." India started crying again. "It's a nightmare."

"But why can't you do the chemotherapy?" I said.

"Because it would kill me sooner than the tumour, and in any case leave me shrivelled, hairless and far more uncomfortable than I am at the moment. It is not a survivable cancer. You know that. The entire world knows that. The rare few make it, but they end up with calcified nodules in their brains and have to take anti-seizure medication for the rest of their lives and wear glasses that make their eyes seem three sizes too big. I'm already losing my memory. I ran into someone in the lobby of our hotel last night who greeted me fondly, and I couldn't even remember who she is. I simply stared at her like a moron. She certainly didn't look like anyone I would ever have befriended. She had blue hair. My life is over."

Sindy appeared to take our orders, just as India put her face in her hands and sobbed and I put an arm around her shoulder.

"Maybe a round of Brouilly," I said, "and some toast points with *foie gras*?"

Sindy nodded, turned and went in pursuit of sustenance.

"Mind you, my oncologist is about as sexy as they come. I know you're curious. He probably has to shave three times a day, at least."

I massaged India's neck, desperately searching for what to say – had society evolved an etiquette for these situations? "You are a brilliant artist and nothing can change that. Your sculpture 'The Arm' –?"

"Yes," India said. "Summer of 2002 – it's in Stanley Park now, in Vancouver."

"When I saw it, I was amazed by the manner in which the woman's finger points toward," I concentrated and finally settled on, "infinity."

"Did you read that somewhere?"

"*India.*"

"I don't mean to insult you – but, really?"

"Well, I am insulted and, yes, really. Hamish and I attended a presentation on modern sculptors at the Pompidou last year and they had replicas on display. 'The Arm' was one of them. And I wasn't the only one who admired it."

"I'll be damned," India said. "I thought you were playing me – saying something to take my mind off my impending demise. Many people miss the finger entirely."

"How could they?"

"I don't know." India shook her head – and then we shared a look of dismay at peoples' aesthetic insensitivities. "I forever have to mention it. You're one of the first who has seen it straight away. It looks beautiful in place, by the way – though I don't imagine one wants to take a trip to British Columbia just to see it."

I shrugged, as if such an idea seemed inspiring. "I have always been in awe of you," I said; then blushing I added, "And I love you."

A long silence shadowed our table.

"I'm a tad speechless at that," India said, looking closely at me, an ersatz son who had never given her a word of praise that she could remember.

I looked back at her in some true surprise. The words uttered themselves. Perhaps my angels *had* hithered hence.

"Thanks, Lovey," she said.

Sindy arrived with the wine and *foie gras*, and flashed us a smile; the lifting of our mood – however false and temporary – must have been evident.

"By the way," I said, "speaking of the Pompidou, I read that they had recently purchased one of your pieces."

"They did?"

"You didn't know?"

India reflected. "Well, it may be the piece Ronald's gallery sold last month. I wish I'd known, I'd happily have been throwing it in Balfour's face. I mean, really – Pompidou trumps copycat murderers in Wyoming. Bloody Hell, if it's Ronald's piece then they paid an absolute fortune for the thing."

"The Pompidou doesn't do auctions well," I said. "They always look too eager."

"Eagerness is not good strategy for auctions – or romance. I rather like the idea of being in the Pompidou."

"So you should. Eagerness may not be a good strategy, but it doesn't spoil what comes after."

"Aren't you witty? If you'd like me to put in a good word with my oncologist – I know you like a bit on the side from time to time."

I put my arm around her shoulder again. "I'm so very sorry."

"I've wanted to carry on, you know – not to discuss it, because I wanted people to think that I was strong and capable."

"Which you are."

"Which I am not," India said, "I'm a depressed, middle-aged woman sitting despondently in a French restaurant. Perhaps I should just sit here popping Xanax and morphine for several hours, avoiding an anxiety attack and – unsuccessfully – the snoopy eyes of some woman staring down at us from a third-floor apartment, behind that balcony filled with half-dead flowers."

I looked up; something rustled.

"Did you really not know?" She asked. "Théophile said nothing?"

"Would I have kept silent if he had? No, not a word. Perhaps another Kir?" I asked, gently kissing her cheek. "I'm sure we can have Sindy roll us out to a taxi after."

India stood up. "No, I think I'll take a walk," she said. "But thank you, Justin."

"I'd like to see the sculpture – in place, as you say – even if I have to go to British Columbia."

"Vancouver has fabulous Chinese restaurants," India said. "In addition to good sculpture."

"And I love Szechuan duck."

"With shrimp dumplings to start?"

"*Voilà*."

Théophile had just left for the gym – or tennis or soccer – so when the doorbell rang, I leapfrogged over the ottoman and pulled the door open.

"*Marigold?*"

"Clever you."

"You're standing in what looks like red-eyed despair on my landing. Are you looking for my legendary hangover cure?"

"No, though I should take the recipe. We need to talk."

"Let's go for a walk, then" I said. "Théophile's off doing one of his testosterone things and, I could do with getting out of here." I grabbed my keys from the table by the door and pulled it shut behind me. Together, we walked down the stairs, through the first courtyard, out through the second courtyard, then through the carriage entrance to the street.

"So," I said, as we came out on the pavement and started walking. "Your mother has brought me to speed on her impending death, and I'm mortified that no one thought to tell me before this and Javier has informed me that I'm a destructive influence on Ham and that I should break up with him, I guess you'd say. In fact, I more or less gather that he's taken charge of smashing our friendship."

"Yes, I know," Marigold said.

I looked at her.

"Don't give me that face," she said. "Everyone knows how horrible the last years have been for you, lovey. But, nonetheless, you have rather squelched our Hamish, don't you think?

The shoe's been waiting to drop for a long time. Javier just hurried it along."

"*Squelched?* That's a bit over the top." I looked at her to see if she really meant it; she did. "Actually, Marigold, I think I've offered something good for Ham. I know I can be sassy, but I mean well."

"Do you?"

That knocked me. I felt nonplussed. We always say we mean well, and I'd done it spontaneously. However, whether I really did mean well had never crossed my mind. At best, I suppose I had never meant anything wicked in my sassiness. Did that count as squelching? If so, a Hell of a lot of squelched people wandered the streets. Perhaps they did? For a moment, I felt as if I were falling, as I did when I took too many Xanax and Clonazepam and my blood pressure bottomed out. Everything blurred and through the unexpected haze I wondered if I even *liked* Hamish. Had I ever liked him? How did you judge these things?

"Javier loves Hamish," Marigold said

That struck me as a non-sequitur; how did Javier get back in?

"What?" she asked, when I looked cross. "You don't want Javier to love him, because you've never wanted anyone to love him, even though Hamish needs – desperately needs – to be loved. It's been merely a matter of time before he found someone who –" but she left the sentence incomplete.

"I'm hardly an ogre. For fuck's sake."

She shook her head in disagreement. "You're not even nice to him."

"I'm not?"

She stopped on the sidewalk and stared at me again. We resumed walking.

"At least neither one of us is crying," Marigold said. "Mind you, we're both over the legal limit for operating a vehicle."

"Why would *you* be crying in public," I asked.

"Missing my husband and children? Distress over my mother's situation?" She waved her hand in the Chatterton fashion. "You know, I think Javier is good for Hamish. He's honest and – you know? Decent. Faithful."

"All of the things that I'm not?"

"Like the rest of my family, I'm thrilled to see Hamish feel loved, and finally not to be running from it – despite your best efforts."

"Despite my best efforts," I echoed, feeling betrayed by everyone and everything, and yet feeling a sting of truth. "Good for Hamish, then."

We entered a nineteenth-century Arcade and passed a Tabac with racks of postcards outside the door. I squinted at her, making my confused face. "You said you wanted to talk; but we haven't talked, you've simply endorsed my separation from Hamish. Was that why you came over?"

She offered me nothing.

Since she didn't say anything more – my question hung there like smoke. We walked on in silence. With each step, it became a more uncomfortable silence, singular, unkempt, not the silence between friends; the echo of our footfalls on the tile floor sounded disturbing. Both of us burst to say something yet knew it couldn't be said. The air around us began to feel electric, like those balls in science class that make your hair stand straight up. When we emerged back out on the street, we nearly collided with a family of tourists, mother, father, and two children, carrying plastic sacks from the trinket stands by the Holiday Inn.

This almost crash seemed to discharge the electrical undercurrent.

"Oh my God, those socks," Marigold said.

The tourist man looked at his feet. His wife and children looked at his feet.

"This isn't some bloody beach in Spain," Marigold said. "It's the bloody middle of Paris. Why are you wearing shorts and those, those – *those socks?*"

The man looked down again at his feet, then up at me, as if for assistance.

His wife looked around nervously.

The children stared, riveted by the unfolding drama.

"Really, I can't take it," Marigold said, nearly crying, and shrieking now, her voice wailing as if she were in pain. "I can't, Justin – I just can't. Just leave Hamish the fuck alone, now and forever. That's it, pure and simple."

"And yet you came all this way for my birthday. Hardly pure and certainly not simple."

"And bloody expensive to boot," she said turning on her heel and walking away.

I looked at the completely disconcerted tourist people. "It's hell turning thirty," I said. "I'm sure you agree."

7

"Are you going to jump?" I asked. "I considered it myself this morning."

Campbell turned from where he stood at the window in his boxer shorts. "I'd have to slither out of this thing like a snake, so no. How – ?"

I waggled the key card. "A boy has his ways."

We stared at one another a long while.

"And a boy used his ways because – ?"

"Because I want you to make mad passionate love to me. That's why. I've been wanting you to ravish me since that kiss on the Rue de Rivoli."

Campbell smiled. "You're crazy."

"Quite likely. Come on," I said, "let's do it."

"And Théophile –?"

"You want him to join us?"

"I meant, despite all of the – well, you're still his – well, shit, Justin."

I had moved closer to Campbell until he seized my face and kissed me passionately.

"But I don't –" he said, as I ran a hand up his chest and then down beneath the elastic of his boxers, where he had a substantial erection.

"Ah, my old friend," I said.

"This is all wrong, despite your old friend's willing welcome." He had a breathy passion he couldn't hide.

"Why are you so nervous about a healthy session of lovemaking?" I asked, my lips tender against his neck. He let me remove his boxers and then he stood before me naked. I put my head against his chest hair, saying, "I love your chest, I always have. It kind of feels like home."

"Okay," Campbell said, nuzzling and kissing me, "I guess it's kind of like a temporary home," then picking me up, he tossed me on the bed, perfectly – I landed on my back, head on a pillow, limbs outstretched. I had forgotten Campbell's flinging-around talents. Then, with smooth, seductive efficiency, he undressed me and did indeed ravish me with proficiency and precision, to my screamfully clawing delight, with waves of orgasm. Had anything ever felt so enjoyable, I wondered, like nourishment, as essential as food and water? And then it was over and we lay side-by-side, sweating and breathing hard.

"Amazing," I said, as I closed my eyes and rested my head in the crook of his shoulder.

"Amazing," Campbell said back, kissing my forehead and holding me closer in our sweaty cocoon.

We drifted off to sleep – obviously – because I still felt Campbell's sweaty warmth, even as we rode down the Boulevard Malesherbes in a car with tinted windows. Peculiar flashings of recognizable landmarks seemed to light up the interior; Campbell drove and I saw Hamish sitting in the front passenger seat, while I rested naked in someone's arms. *Whose?* I definitely felt aroused and safe, at least until the car began to skid and jolt. Suddenly I lurched forward, as Campbell sat up in bed, and I awoke to the gruff sound of Théophile's voice:

"… and I need to take you to the hospital immediately. We tried ringing the hotel phone as well, but," and he gestured to where it lay buried beneath clothes, "clearly you couldn't hear it."

Campbell had by now leapt from bed and frantically began to dress.

I looked at Théophile and a stony-faced hotel employee behind him. "What – ?"

"I'm taking Campbell to the hospital. You can find a taxi or call a service."

Campbell buttoned his jeans and, realizing that I had missed the crucial part of the conversation, told him, "My mother had a heart attack."

"Full cardiac arrest," Théophile said, "in Luxembourg Garden. They fished her out of the flowers and reanimated her, but I'm afraid that it doesn't look good."

"*Oh, my God,*" I said. "And you mean resuscitate in English."

"Yes, yes. Come along," Théophile said, as Campbell stuffed his wallet into his front pocket.

I watched them turn their backs on me and leave. I stared at the door, then I burst into tears, rolled over and – burying my face in Campbell's pillow – sobbed with heaving gasps.

I knew well the nudgings of a panic attack, this somnambulistic sense of doom, sweaty palms, a sense of impending death. As I came into the waiting room I saw from Hamish's quick glance at me that something had gone amiss in my dressing. I looked down and saw the buttons out of sync on my shirt. I left them. No one spoke to me, nor I to them, I simply stood near the vending machine, sweating. Bridges on fire everywhere tonight, I thought. Javier, in a form-fitting T-shirt beneath an open Lacoste dress shirt, held Hamish as he cried against his chest. Marigold sat holding hands with Théophile; she gave me a passing glance, then spoke softly to Théophile. Balfour and Campbell sat together by a potted tree. Nicolas, looking as if he too had dressed in a hurry, sat by himself in the corner. He must have driven Marigold, I thought, as my vision grew impressionistic, colours blurred: doom crept closer. My rejection felt excruciating; even Javier and Théophile sat included in the family circle, Théophile like an ersatz Carwyn.

I sat next to Nicolas, who put his arm around my shoulder. It helped – *some*. Nothing could stop a panic attack this severe except several Xanax or Clonazepam, and I had neither; I had only sleep-musky Nicolas. Curled under Nicolas's arm, I slipped like Alice down the rabbit hole, back to the horrendous Bataclan night, Théophile and me attempting to navigate Paris with its roadblocks, soldiers, police, speeding ambulances, trying to find the hospital with Didier and Benoît. Mobile phones weren't working, but we had gone by their apartment and knew they had not been home. Sometime after the second or third hospital – and endless waiting in clammy crowds of parents, brothers, sisters, friends, that gave off an odour of dread – a sudden flurry of messages burst forth on my phone from both Didier and Benoît's parents. Nothing arrived from either Didier or Benoît; from them, only silence.

We searched until dawn and beyond.

I saw myself there again, now drenched in sweat, heart pounding, afraid to move, clinging to Nicolas, remembering how a doctor came to speak to us about Benoît, catalogued in the morgue – and although I knew this doctor spoke of India, the click, click, click of sharp images snapping in my head were of me finding Benoît in the morgue and identifying his greyish-yellow face. Didier had been so mutilated that they found it difficult to reconstruct his body. Although I clearly saw the movement in the room, saw weeping, saw despair, the molten heat of my skin seemed to have melted my clothes, which dripped my sweat on Nicolas. Clearly, I saw Didier across the room, although I knew that Hamish stood there in Javier's arms, not Didier – and yet, he wore Didier's face, and he bled, he bled. I let go of Nicolas and tried to stand up, to reach out to Didier, but I fell – hard – and lay there fully conscious, aware that my bladder had lost its hold and my urine grew in a pool; aware of Nicolas kneeling and calling for a nurse, aware, with cinematic clarity – just before I lost consciousness – of Marigold saying, "It's fucking all about him, even when our mother has just died."

In those last conscious moments, I knew that Nicolas knelt beside me and that he checked for a peripheral pulse and opened the collar of my shirt. Through a fog darkly – or whitely – I saw my extraordinarily colourless hand and arm, almost translucent. Then Nicolas pulled up his shirtsleeves, took me into his arms, stood up, and moved down the hall past Marigold and Théophile, toward the nursing station.

I awoke slowly, crying, although I knew neither why I cried nor on top of whose bed I lay stretched out in my underwear. Turning my head, which ached, I saw across a large courtyard. Groggily I remembered – *everything*. I stared at the elaborate plaster motif around the ceiling. For a while I tried to think only of the plaster; it proved impossible. I rolled on my side. Though I had to sit up to do it – and that made me lightheaded – I poured myself a glass of water. Of course, in Nicolas's apartment, a bottle of Wattwiller water and a glass would thoughtfully have been left beside the bed. I downed the water in a gulp. When my dizziness dissipated, I stood up and, searching the wardrobe, found a stack of my T-shirts – neatly folded – along with shorts and a selection of summery footwear. Once dressed, I went down the hall where – not surprisingly, since she had been the guest here before me – I found Marigold reading a novel. She put it down as she heard me come into the room.

"You're as white as a sheet," Marigold said. "Do you want something to eat?"

"No. All of my clothes are here."

"It was quite the performance. Nicolas hired an army. Truck loads are stored in the rooms next door to you. It's the French way. Théophile is anticipating your lawyer's demand for a fair '*partager*,' so anything even vaguely connected to you has been sent over here – and Théophile and his family are guarding their patrimony like the hounds of Hell. I shouldn't imagine that in terms of tangible property you'll get anything else besides what's over here, which is considerable – I didn't know you owned a Gauguin, by the way. The lawyers can haggle over money in bank accounts, but unless the two of you bought any property together, it will all go to Théophile. Did you take his name when you married? If so, you shan't be able to keep it."

"Thank you for your precision, Marigold." I sat in one of the fauteuils. "The Gauguin was a gift from an infatuated lover, and I don't have a lawyer yet, but once I do, I'm certain he or she will know all the arcane French squiggles."

Marigold looked away from me, out the window toward the afternoon sunlight on the facades of Rue de Thann.

"You're angry? About me and Campbell? It may have ruined my marriage, but that's about all it accomplished. There's nothing between us and now – well, even our friendship's ruined."

She nodded.

"How's Hamish?"

She turned to me. "Javier is taking care of him." Then, "Do you suppose she caused it by her drugs and drinking? Or was it just the brain tumour?"

"Is that what – I mean, doesn't the hospital have a definitive, you know – ?"

"Not yet."

"Look, Marigold. I'm not excusing myself or having regrets, because that's stupid – and I have a pounding headache. It's hard to be maudlin with a near-migraine. But the truth is that I haven't been the same since – well, you know I have PTSD, and that it's changed everything. I've been clinically depressed, which is part of it, of course. The medication warps you as well as helps you. Apparently, clonazepam does something to the structure of your brain. Anyway, I did something stupid, I had sex with Campbell, it's about number two-thousand on the list of stupid things I've done since Didier and Benoît died at the Bataclan. Maybe I was better off when I was in that creepy never-leave-the-house period. Anyway, I'm not the person you used to know; I never will be again."

I paused a moment and held my head in my hands; I felt as if it might burst.

"Oddly, I have some kind of clarity at the moment," I said. "Don't ask me why. The famous Margaret Thatcherite short, sharp shock? But if I can get this headache to subside and – well, fuck it – ."

Marigold left the room and came back with several capsules and some water. "You're meant to take these," she said. "They'll blast away the migraine."

I gulped them down with the water. "Look, Marigold, I – "

"Bloody Hell," she said, nearly running to the window, "Shut up, already Justin."

I sat, stunned, staring at her back, feeling the unknown pills sizzle in my head and stomach.

"I'm sick of your fucking narcissism," she said.

"*What?*"

She looked at me, turned quickly away and stared again out the window.

"Marigold?"

Nothing.

"*Marigold?*"

"What?" she said, hard-toned, without turning around.

"What *what?*"

She stood silently, offering me a continuing view of her back. I remained silent, settling back into the chair. A clock ticked maddeningly. Water ran somewhere. Far off pipes gurgled.

"Is this because Théophile found Campbell screwing me?" I asked, feeling angry now and hurt, "That was stupid, it was wrong. But we all do stupid things – like date guys with fused earlobes and white South African policeman and then run off with Welsh surfers."

She turned and gave me a furious look.

"I loved India," I said, and my voice quavered. "If I've had a real mother, I guess it's been her." My eyes teared up.

"Oh, yeah, right," Marigold said, rounding on me. "India was a meal ticket, a name you could drop, hardly a mother. It's laughable. All you've ever done is take advantage of her, of us – Campbell – Hamish – our family. *Fuck you, Justin.*"

We stared at one another, and something in me both exploded and imploded. This felt like the most centred moment since Bataclan; it also felt as if I became someone new, still Justin – and yet not Justin. Turning thirty felt unimportant, and the shambles of my marriage seemed somehow – what? Appropriate. I closed my eyes, and when I opened them, I

heard my own voice – altered, cold, and yet perhaps more ma-
ture, "Big change from a few days ago in my living room, snug-
gling and weeping your sympathy for me. I've never trusted big
changes like this. Have you?" Before she could answer, I said,
"And a meal ticket? To what? Some Addams family-style buffet?
You're a family of kooks. And at best you've only ever tolerated
me, you wonderful Bedminsters, which I've known the whole
time, by the way. I was just putting on that jabber-jaw happy-
go-lucky bullshit in order to feel like I belonged, to pretend
like maybe I *did* have a family. Yet none of you really cared
that I needed a psychiatrist to give me drugs to keep me from
killing myself, I was so shit miserably desperate."

"You told us often enough. I think we knew."

"Why is this about me? Campbell, okay, I was wrong. As
for Hamish, I've been a good friend – in my way, because he's
as odd a duck as the rest of you. Jesus, Marigold, I remember
you hanging around me laughing and carrying on like some
freaking oddball all of those summers and winter breaks. Hell,
I even remember you *admiring* my morning erection once."

"Yes. I recall the morning. Mother sent me in to wake you
up. I wasn't used to the sort of guests who didn't wear pyjamas,
so I wasn't sure what to say when a guest in our home displayed
his prominently mounted erection," she snapped.

I could think of nothing to say; I said nothing.

Marigold continued to glare at me.

In the end, I stood up – stunning myself with my pent-up
anger, "You're a fucking fake, Marigold. Congratulations on
carrying it off. You were an irritating piece of shit back in the
day, coming into my bedroom uninvited, talking about crap,
inviting yourself to parties Hamish and I were going to, and –
yeah – I hated that. Frankly, I have absolutely no idea how I really feel about you – except that at this moment I think you're

as manipulative a bitch as my mother was." I shook a finger at her, and I watched it tremble, so angry had I become. "You practically *ruined* one entire winter break, hanging around me and Campbell, when you knew I was in love with him, you were always there – some goofy nerd with dyed hair and Goth outfits. I didn't take advantage of a damn thing and you – you were an asshole whom *I tolerated*."

She merely shrugged.

"Tolerating you had to be some kind of affection, I suppose, because like everyone else in your family – the one I was apparently taking advantage of – I thought you were off your rocker."

She made a spitting sound, touching her fingers to an imaginary radiator and making a sizzling noise. "Feel better?"

"Oh, for the love of – *whatever*."

"Usually, God, but what they hey – let's say 'for the love of Princess Diana.' Wasn't she a gay icon?"

We looked daggers at one another.

"I wrote a poem once about how you and Hamish treated me,' she said, "it was published, in fact – though not in any of those magazines with half naked men in thongs and handcuffs so I doubt you or Campbell or Hamish or Théophile read it."

A long, far too long, pause snuffed out the room's air.

"How *I* treated *you?*"

"You heard correctly. I was having frozen yogurt at the mall, when you, Campbell, Hamish and some friends traipsed by my table. You saw me – we all knew you saw me. I had a mouth full of Butter Pecan yogurt, so I couldn't say anything. But I thought *you* would. You didn't. Pretending not to see me, which was one big *unfunny* joke, you and my brothers and friends just walked away. I stayed with my yogurt, which was melting anyway. It's titled "My Brother's Friend Having Ignored Me."

To be ignored is cruel
Irony, which plays
Insecurity
Against itself in a
Destructive duel of
Desire. And no
Retaliation,
Since you must exist
To seek your revenge,
And denial is
Vengeless cold longing.

"Such an amazing memory for such an execrably forget-table – well, I'll go ahead and call it a poem, for the sake of good manners," I said, thinking it merely an exercise in self-pity – something I recognized, inasmuch as self-pity and I had an intimate acquaintance. "Fuck you all to Hell and back, Marigold – you and everyone else in your hare-brained family. Oh, and while I'm thinking of it, you can have every damn one of your fucking angels back – except for Gloria Swanson, I'm keeping Gloria Swanson," then I turned left the room.

To my mind, few places have the beauty of the Vendée at sunset. In the event you don't know, it's a French Department, in the middle of France in the West, famed for many things, like melons, marshes, canals and staying loyal to the crown during the Revolution (not a wise move, as it turned out). I love how the countryside spreads out smoothly with blue-green rivers passing beneath Napoleonic bridges (Napoleon liked the Vendee, for a reason I've forgotten – their weird un-bending loyalty, no doubt), beside the melon fields that made the Province rich.

Often on a sunny summer evening, when we were visiting his family, Théophile jogged shirtless on the path leading to the river, and I watched him as he ran. Occasionally, I caught up to him after he reached his evening spot, as he leaned over to catch his breath, and then we stood peaceably on the bank of the Vendée River, watching the descending sun glint off the water as it gurgled over stones and through the reeds. Grey-blue shadows would intensify into green woodlands and fields, silhouettes spread into trees, grew branches and let loose chattering flocks of scarlet and white birds. All of that in the past now, like the end of a school year and knowing you'll never seen your third-grade classroom again – and not knowing which fourth grade teacher or classroom you would have.

"Life has either too much or too little meaning," I said, to whoever lay beside me on the bed.

"Perhaps, it is we who give it too much or too little meaning," Nicolas said.

"Oh, hello," I said, turning so that I could face him.

"Théophile's lawyer rang. He wants to know if it will signify if he comes to the funeral. And Campbell has sent over a message to you. A letter."

"May I have some water?" Then, "Oh, God, Nicolas, I've wet the bed."

"Here," Nicolas said, handing me the water. "And not to worry about the bed. I will have it changed and the *matelas* dried, cleaned and reversed while we are having our dinner."

Having nursed the mineral water, I lay back down beside Nicolas, ignoring the unpleasant smell of urine. "I'll have a look at Campbell's letter in my next life – or not. And what does the lawyer mean? *Signify?*"

"In France, matters of divorce can be tricky."

I tried to think about that. "Like, does it mean we're reconciled if we both go to India's funeral?"

Nicolas made a confused face. "It is a lawyer matter and I don't know much about the fine points – but yes."

"How silly," I said. "I think I remember Marigold saying something about all of my earthly possessions having been trucked over here."

"Théophile seemed in the rush to have them removed."

"Probably preparing to install someone new."

"Yes, that is correct," Nicolas said, "and that is most certainly something for your lawyer to verify with a *hussier*. I know a good one."

I turned and looked again at Nicolas. "He's been having an affair. And you and everyone else has known about it."

"Yes."

"How fucking embarrassing. Why didn't anyone tell me?"

Nicolas pursed his lips, but seemed either unable to find the words or unwilling to speak them.

I sighed, "That's what the big talk after my birthday was going to be about. And yet another shoe drops."

"*Finir ce que l'on a commence*," Nicolas said.

"Something like that. Look. I don't give a flying fuck if Théophile goes to the funeral or not – *I'm* terrified about going, facing all of them. Quite frankly, I don't want to see any of them ever again, especially not Hamish – not until I've talked that out with my shrink. I loved India, she was a mother figure, more like my real mother than I chose to see. I should honor that. Right? But I'm finished with the rest of them." I turned and looked at Nicolas. "By the way, I have no lawyer, and once I do I don't think I want him or her probing anything. There must be some fast track."

"Ah, no, *hélas* – not yet in France. I shall find you a good lawyer and we will let him do as he sees fit. That is his profession." Nicolas looked a long while at me "You are really finished with Hamish?"

I kept the look with Nicolas. "I wasn't given a choice, Nicolas. And has *he* sent me a message?"

"No. But, his mother has just died and he is grieving."

"True, but Javier and Marigold made clear that I'm persona non-grata in Hamish's life. Apparently, I'm a destructive influence. We've always had an *odd* friendship. And – well, I'll see how I feel in a week or so, perhaps after the emotions of the funeral have settled – *if I go* – but I think it's time for me to move on – from everything." I looked then at the ceiling. "Bad influences often cut both ways."

Nicolas took my hand and held it in his strong, warm grip. "Why don't you shower and change, and then we will eat – and I shall accompany you to the funeral. So, no need to worry further about that. What is the Anglo-Saxon saying? I will have your back."

Coming into the café where I often had lunch – which counted as a ballsy move, all things considered (I'd taken an upper-end Uber and not the bus or metro), the host showed me to my usual table at an open *porte-fenêtre*. I hung my satchel over the back of my chair, as if I'd been at school. I should be working, but given the scrambled eggs I had for emotions, I couldn't make the effort. My decisions might be flawed, and the hubbub of school life would keep me permanently on the edge of a panic attack: I'd need to have my finger on Nicolas's number at all times. As I sat down, I looked out on the Parisian boulevard lined with cafés and nearly identical chairs. The waiter had with practiced surreptitiousness brought my Badoit mineral water. I had been thinking this afternoon about India, whom I had once admired as a woman who had everything:

husband, family, career, wit. She even had those beautiful white teeth everyone favoured. I even loved how, when I asked her about them, she said, 'I paid for them, lovey, the way you do everything in America. Life over there is just one fucking cash transaction.'

Much to my surprise, Campbell sent me a text this morning, apologizing for his part in what he termed our misbehaviour, which sounded as if we had been scamps at boarding school – but clearly signalling that no repeat performances could be scheduled. As if I wanted to. *Please*. He had correctly guessed that I had not read his letter; I deleted the text and tossed the hard copy letter into the rubbish bin in Nicolas's kitchen. Something really had changed since India's death and I wanted to get to the bottom of it. Should I be hospitalized, I wondered? After more death, abandonment and loss, didn't that make sense? Yet, I felt – well, if not better, then certainly on the way toward better. I didn't dare say that out loud – not even to Nicolas – for fear of jinxing things, but I felt it all the same. I examined the daily chalkboard menu a moment, gestured to the waiter and ordered my usual, a *salade rurale* and a glass of Brouilly.

Out the window: a passing set of pedestrians, a fashionable young man and his provincial mother and grandmother. When Théophile and I fell in love – if we really *did* fall in love – we were too young and I too ruthless. I saw that now. I wanted someone with Théophile Legrêle-Chevrier's money and power. My boyfriend Paolo, a magnificent lover, had incipient power – but no money and he would never have power in Théophile's manner. I tore a piece of bread apart and nibbled on some of the soft middle. Clearly, I had not loved Théophile for a long time; I may have pretended, and I may have liked his body, which made me feel safe, but I hadn't loved *him*. His money and power had felt illusory for years, and even more so after Bataclan. I moved my hands so that the waiter could place my salad in front of me. Then, I returned my gaze to the street.

A few weeks ago, school politics demanded that I attend an alumni party in a chic building on the *Avenue de la Grande Armée*, in Neuilly-sur-Seine. I felt well enough to go. From the moment I arrived, however, I felt like an old maid in the hip crowd. I had almost immediately taken some champagne and opened the door to the terrace, with its pots of geraniums, leaving the party behind me – in a skinny apartment crowded with skinny people and skinny unknown foods. Dark Paris night noise erupted as I stepped out to the square perch above the boulevard. I went to the rail and peered at the traffic surging east toward the *Champs* Élysées. Taxis, cars, buses, bicycles, motorcycles, jockeying to the *rond-point*, racing down what were alternately four, five or six lanes of traffic, depending upon the audacity of the drivers. At a bar across the street, a drunken woman shouted in an English accent at a young man with a nice haircut and apologetic gestures. I stood there a long while, thinking about the emotional meltdown at the heart of my life – the dread of the unknown, the smashing of hopes and dreams. Fortuitously, I did not have a panic attack that night; nor did I now as I sat in front of my salad looking out the window, where the city shimmered in summer heat.

Operatic clouds drowsed by; the sidewalks seemed quieter than when I arrived; a trio of young women moved sluggishly along the periphery of my vision. One famous Café, however, had busloads of Chinese tourists thronging it. I never ate there. A woman trained her dog unenthusiastically on a patch of lawn beneath chestnut trees; I recognized her language as Scandinavian. A British Airways plane circled overhead, its muted jet blasts like the war-cry of global warming – about which I had once cared, before my concerns became basic, like staying upright, not making bizarre gurgling noises as I lurched into a panic attack, and not shrieking in sudden terror in a food hall. I left the Great Barrier Reef to others now. I ate my salad and drank my wine, and when I looked again at the sky I saw gathering thunderclouds. The waiters shut the French doors; the musty smell of the restaurant wrapped around me. Raindrops pattered on the pavement.

Inevitably, the home movies of my life began, those cinematic loops that – this time – had been brought up from their vault by India's death. Feeling a tad wobbly, a popped a couple of Lorazepam and ordered another glass of wine. On the pill-popping precipice of thirty, I no longer craved money or power, but stability, peace, safety, warmth – and, yes, *fidelity* – all of the accoutrements of bourgeois life. How in the Hell did that happen? And when? I wanted to be held and loved, touched by loving hands. My heart fluttered, and I could hardly hold the glass in my hand once it arrived. I quickly set it down on the table. The shoe dropped, the mirror cracked; the chair sagged beneath me, like a trap door on a stage set.

My God, I thought.

I had hit bottom and I now headed upward.

8

As Nicolas and I stood surveying St. Hilda's Church in Beacons-field – sussing out the setting for India's funerary pageant – gun shots rang out from a side chapel. Without a second thought, Nicolas leapt toward the chapel, and – after second, third and fourth thoughts, and an electrical sense of impending horror – I followed him. For years, apparently, the chapel had been a refuge of crumbling statuary. When Nicolas opened the door, we faced not determined terrorists, but a row of statues with their crotches blown off, puffing mouldy plaster powder from their mutilated private parts, and a drunk Marigold, standing just inside the chapel staring at us.

Nicolas turned and looked at me – surprised, I think, to realize that I had followed him – but said nothing.

Marigold had lowered the hunting rifle.

"Are you drunken, Marigold?" Nicolas asked

"Yes," she said.

"Very?"

"Perhaps."

"Well, then," he said, moving down the aisle, taking the gun from her and pushing her into sitting beside him on a dusty pew. Once there, he reached around and placed the gun on the pew behind them.

For my part I stood in the nave, watching and listening; I could not muster much empathy for Marigold. Neither did I wish to test the waters of potential panic.

"I don't want to stay awake," Marigold said, "I want to die."

Nicolas looked at her. "I am shocked by this. Anything is better than dying. Am I not correct, Justin?"

Although I paused – considering everything I've learned I'm still not sure one ought to commit to the anything part of it – I could not leave Nicolas in the lurch, so I said, "Sitting in a dark closet staring at mops is better than dying. I know, I've done it – the staring at mops part."

She shrugged. I don't imagine she mustered much empathy for me either, even when liquored up and over emotional.

"Need I to remind you of the five little orphans you would be leaving behind as well as artistically handsome Gareth down under," Nicolas told her.

"I've made huge mistakes," she said drunkenly. "I should have married Nethersole. I miss him. I miss him terribly. I made a mistake."

"Regarding mistakes," Nicolas said. "I would be most certain that I wanted to destroy six innocent lives before I blew out my brains. There is no coming back from *that* mistake."

She leaned her head on his shoulder. "I loved Nethersole."

"Hindsight is twenty-twenty. I am sure he has moved on with his life as well. Perhaps he has five little Nethersoles surfing with him in Cape Town."

"Of course," she said, "you're right. But you don't realize you've taken the wrong path until it's too late."

"I know you love your five *gamins*, and Gareth with the black chest hair, and *mon Dieu*, you have had a most adventuresome life from what Justin recounts to me: working in Africa, farming on a commune in – "

"Upstate New York. Mom and dad financed us, so I'm not sure if it counted as a real commune or not. Mind you, I wasn't there for any kind of communing." She gave him a sly wink. "Lord have mercy, he was a big, broad-chested Adonis, eyes as violet as Elizabeth Taylor's."

I moved a few feet closer to them, suddenly feeling softer toward this crumpled Marigold. "One does love a man with a big chest and violet eyes," I said.

"Amen," she agreed.

"So," I said, glancing at Nicolas. "How's about you agree not to blow your brains out or leap from any windows or take a handful of drugs. Such a waste of time, energy, lives. One can live well enough with suicidal impulses, trust me again. Had you consulted me on the matter, I'd have offered sound advice. Anyway, Nicolas and I would rather stay in England for just one funeral. Sorry to be so selfish."

"You've never apologized before for being selfish."

I thought about that. Does anyone ever apologize for being selfish? That seems such a broad stroke of the brush. She meant the remark sarcastically, of course. "I'm assuming you meant that sarcastically?"

Nicolas gave me a warning look and waggled his finger in the French fashion.

"Well," I said, taking my cue from Nicolas, "put it this way then: the last thing your mother would want to do is share the stage on her Anglican High-Church funeral. *She* never apologized for being selfish either."

Marigold giggled with drunken hiccups and collapsed against Nicolas in a drunken heap.

Nicolas and I found ourselves squeezed into a pew next to India's brother Nathaniel and his wife (the usher really said,

'Miss Chatterton's brother and his wife would like you to join them,' with a practiced wave). Of course, under the circumstances of my break-up with Théophile and Hamish and my hissing cat fight with Marigold, I didn't see how we merited such exalted placement. Someone must have taken one look at Nicolas in his French finery and looked him up in some French aristocratic 'Who's Who.' One had to exist. Presumably, now that I knew him well, he had to rank high on several Who's Who lists. One never knew with Nicolas, the clever sphinx. At any rate, the usher knew *exactly* where to place us. We snooped – since we had no other option – on the conversation between India's brother and sister-in-law.

"Who in the bloody Hell invited *that* ragamuffin?" The sister-in-law demanded of her husband.

Both of us recognized her at the same time: Victoria Carlyle.

I had never known that India and my beautifully eccentric idol Victoria Carlyle were related; in twelve years not India, Hamish, Campbell or Marigold had said a word. All of them knew I worshipped her and yet they said nothing. I felt all of a sudden as if there had to be more – *much more* – from which I had been excluded. Had I ever been part of their in-crowd? Despite the fact that I shared everything – well, nearly everything – with them and introduced my Uncle Irwin to Balfour and had believed the two of them became friends, the intimacy had not been reciprocal. I leaned against Nicolas, as some of my early warnings of anxiety went off: he put his arm around me, and held me close, as if he knew (and perhaps he did) just how deeply this hurt.

"*I* did. I invited her," Uncle Nathaniel said.

"But why on earth –?"

"Victoria, for the love of God – it's my sister Elizabeth. India's sister Elizabeth."

"Oh, dear." Out of vanity, Victoria was not wearing her glasses. She squinted at the thin woman in a bright red ensemble. "Why's your little sister wearing a dress three sizes too big? Don't tell me she bought that thing off the rack."

Her husband sighed, "If you went to visit, you would know that she has been on a weight loss programme. She has fresh meals delivered once a week. It's been quite successful."

"You sound like a barrister."

"I *am* a barrister. Look. I know the two of you made a vow not to speak to one another 'ever again,' which I thought at the time was idiotic, although I admit that trip to the Galapagos was ghastly – but India and Elizabeth always loved one another, they had a very special relationship."

They did? This certainly came as news to me. I could remember no mention, other than something cursory perhaps, of India's sister Elizabeth.

"All of those stories about camping up in the Lake District. Your parents did not raise their daughters to go camping in the Lake District, I can tell you that. People have always said she had lesbian tendencies, haven't they?"

"What people say about any of us wouldn't bear repeating in a church. And what on earth is wrong with having lesbian tendencies? Or actually *being* lesbian? You would make a drop-dead gorgeous lesbian, my love." Another sigh. "I think Elizabeth looks absolutely splendid several stones lighter."

"You don't go to a funeral wearing red, lesbian or not," Victoria said. I wouldn't, if I were the leader of the drop-dead lesbians of the United Kingdom. Which I would be. "It's just not done."

"Perhaps she merely wants to see India buried, in the colour of her choosing."

Victoria laughed. "And rejoice in the fact that she doesn't have to contrive excuses for the two of them not to speak about that horrid family of India's. Good God, what a harvest of two-headed tomatoes that group is: just look at them over there."

"Yes, yes, don't let's repeat the whole damn thing."

"I shall repeat as I feel repeating is required, and don't take a tone with me, Nathaniel."

They stared at one another.

Satisfied, Victoria went on. "Whatever is she trying to do?"

"Who?"

"Elizabeth, in that hideous red thing, that's hanging off her like a – what are those Hawaiian things they all wear because they're fat? Mumus?"

"I have no idea what you're talking about, but I believe Elizabeth is greeting people. She's always had a people personality."

"*People personality,*" Victoria growled under her breath. Then she turned to Nicolas. "Hello, handsome. You look familiar."

"Nicolas Perrault."

"So delightfully French." She eyed him from head to toe in a practiced fashion. "You're at least six feet two inches, aren't you? You do stand out."

"I am one metre ninety-two," Nicolas said, glancing at me as if for help. I shrugged. The Marigold episode had depleted my reserves; the two Xanax I had taken, combined with the increasingly bizarre circumstances of India's funeral, left me lopsided.

"*So honest.* It speaks well of your mother. The de-Neandearthalization of men is entirely due to the rigorous training of their mothers. But mind, a man like you needn't fudge the details, amn't I right, Nicolas Perrault? You're not five feet seven or something equally dwarfish. Temptation gets the better of men who are five feet seven. They are always going to be five feet seven *and a half.* Nicolas, if you would be so kind, could you ask that woman in red over there to sit down and stay put."

Nicolas looked as if she had slapped him. "*Pardon?*" His elegant French sounded like the ting of silver against a champagne flute.

"And beware, she has an odour. It's all the diet drugs she takes; they give off the smell of an oil refinery."

"*Oh, for the love of God,*" Nathaniel said, loudly enough for the people behind them to hear. He stood, slid out of the pew and went over to Elizabeth. He pulled her into a hug, and the two of them talked for several minutes – until, in fact, Nathaniel showed her to her seat.

Victoria leaned over to Nicolas and me. "You couldn't pay me to sit over there. Helen Franklin, on the vestry, says there is toxic mould on that column."

Returning to them, Nathaniel said, "She smells deliciously of Clive Christian perfume.

"How in God's name does she afford that?"

A third sigh. A long pause. Then, Nathaniel asked, looking at the order of service, "Who chose these hymns? Good God, they're from the Middle Ages."

"I chose them. Our Anglican Communion dates from the Renaissance, as well you know – and don't tell me how to be Church of England, Mr. Nathaniel Chatterton."

"I hadn't planned on it. However, I've tended to think of you as a more forward-thinking woman than would be implied by "All Glory Laud and Honour to Thee Redeemer King."

"*Oh,*" she said in surprise. "Well, you do have your moments, Nate."

"It is an interesting hymn, historically speaking," Nicolas told us, becoming his sincere and educative self. "Theodulf, Bishop of Orléans wrote the *paroles* in perhaps 820, so it is from the Middle Ages, you are correct *Monsieur* Chatterton, and it was translated into English by a most peculiar man named John Mason Neale, from a family of extremely asserted Evangelicals."

Victoria stared at Nicolas a moment in awe, and then winked at me. "I regret my choice already, but alas there is no changing it now." After patting Nicolas's leg and giving me another wink, she turned her attention back to the assembled wedding guests. "Nate, this – unseemly spectacle, India's demise on a Paris street amongst ordinary tourists, her weird wild children. We need to talk."

"About what?"

"Of many things: Of shoes – and ships – and sealing-wax – Of cabbages – and kings – And why the sea is boiling hot – And whether pigs have wings."

"But wait a bit – the Oysters cried, before we have our chat; for some of us are out of breath –"

"I believe the next line is 'And all of us are fat,'" Victoria said with a quick smile, "So perhaps we should leave off our literary allusion there, Mr. Smarty Pants." And she tapped Nicolas's leg again in happy conspiracy.

I thought that Nicolas had never looked more miserable; it seemed confirmed when he took hold of my hand, and clutched it in his lap, not – I could tell – as comfort to me, but as comfort to him.

"All right," Nate said. "But I love 'The Walrus and the Carpenter'. It's from *Alice through the Looking-Glass*, though I prefer 'Jabberwocky'."

"I have no opinion on that matter," Victoria shrugged. "It's never yet been necessary to have one. Is it necessary, do you think?" She asked Nicolas and me.

"I suppose not," I said, in a bid to shield Nicolas – who, for all I knew, might veer off into a nervous recitation of the history of Lewis Carroll and his predilection for young girls.

"Thank you. And *you* know full well what we need to talk about." She said to Nathaniel, giving him one of her take-no-prisoners looks. Then, glancing across the church she said in mock horror, "Surely Balfour didn't invite *those* girls. The cousins. I mean, honestly. He's gone too far. Those girls should stay indoors and write poetry, like Emily Dickinson, or incomprehensible novels like those Bronte sisters – or else, much more sensibly, have their faces done over with cosmetic surgery. I've said as much to their mother." She sighed, and looked at Nicolas, who had by now lost all colour. "I mean, it's not as if they can't afford it. And what kind of Mayfair mother lets her daughters go through life looking like Godzilla? I ask you?"

I had filled my plate with food from the buffet and gone looking for somewhere quiet to eat. On the second floor, I sat down on the rug in a guest room when Campbell suddenly whooshed down beside me. He must have been following. I took a bite of roast beef, and washed it down with champagne before saying, "I thought you weren't speaking to me. The rest of your family will yellow card you."

"A soccer allusion?"

"I'm branching out."

"Clearly. Hamish is hiding, Balfour is battling with India's family over art work, and Marigold's gone slinking off to Heathrow in the hope of catching the first flight to Oz. She slept through the funeral here in the house. Oh, and Javier is making nice with both sides of the family."

"Big spring wedding planned?"

Campbell laughed and shrugged; I took that as a yes.

"He's made it clear that I'm not to darken Hamish's doorway or gossip with him over catered funeral food – which is harsh and hard, not making nice."

"But we're still friends," Campbell said.

"No," I told him, "We're not. We're acquaintances now, Campbell. You're going to carry on with your life in New York or Los Angeles or wherever you live and I'll never see you. We are past tense."

"But good past tense?"

"The past is what it is," I shrugged. "I seem to have accumulated a surprising amount of past, as well as a superb pharmacological knowledge."

Campbell picked at his food, not putting up any fight for friendship. He ate an olive. "I've tried to be there for you."

"Be where for me?"

"I mean, I've tried to support you – you know, after your mom and Bâtaclan."

I thought about what he said, as best I could, since the effect of champagne and Xanax made concentration unpleasant. I ate some more of the delicious roast beef and small roasted potatoes. "Maybe. If you have to declare it, then – ?"

He gulped some champagne. "You've always been the alpha in our friendship, Justin, the boss, the one who took charge. I've been in your shadow and I've done your bidding."

"Like the other day?"

"Yes."

"You could have told me to get lost and slammed the door in my face, and *you* have always the dominant part of our friendship – at least whenever you wanted to be."

Again, he picked at his food.

"I think it's easier for Javier and Marigold and the rest of your familial gypsy troupe to blame me," I said, "than to blame themselves for Hamish's low self-esteem. My God, don't you wonder why he's drawn to a man like Javier? Javier's like spackle, covering up all the empty holes in Hamish's life with his hyper-virility." I drank the last of my champagne. "You know, this is the best funeral buffet I've ever eaten. Mind you, I think it's my *first* funeral buffet, but really it's delicious."

A long, slinky silence crept between us.

"I'm the one in this group who's lost," Campbell whispered.

"I know," I said. "And I'm totally found. I'm just mentally ill."

Walking back to the hotel along the footpath, I heard someone approach from behind. Turning, I recognized Nicolas by the glow of his white shirt. As he came closer, I saw that he had – since leaving the reception – rolled up his sleeves and unbuttoned more of his collar.

"Miss Carlyle indicated that you had gone again to the hotel," he said.

"You were looking for me?"

"Yes."

"Why?"

"Since I had not seen you in some whereas – "

I paused on the dusky path. "Whereas – *what?*" I wondered, having waited for the end of the quirky sentence.

"I mean to say while. Sorry. Too much to drink, and English is difficult when I am drunken," Nicolas sighed.

"*Pouvions-nous parler français?*"

"No. We stay with English. I had not seen you in some while and I wanted to – see you."

"Oh. Okay, then," I said. "And what? Was Miss Carlyle spying on me?"

"I believe so, yes. I saw her watching you the entire time. It was somewhat embarrassing for me, however. When I inquired about you, she was arguing with Mr. Balfour Bedminster about family matters and I had to interrupt them."

"I guess you really did want to find me."

"Yes. I really did."

"What were they arguing about?"

"India Chatterton's will – and the fact that she wished to have returned to Mr. Bedminister several pieces that she had loaned to Miss Victoria Carlyle's offices in London. Apparently, Miss Carlyle is claiming that they were gifts and is threatening solicitors. However, it seems that Mr. Bedminister has the paperwork affirming only a loan."

"You should have been a spy. A French 007."

"No," Nicolas said, "I could never be someone like that, and those big-breasted bikini women would be wasted upon me."

I laughed.

A gust of warm summer wind filled up Nicolas's white shirt like a sail, flapping the material. "Javier and Hamish were also quarrelling about the correct time to leave," Nicolas said equably, "'which seems somewhat – precious? Fussy? Yes?"

"I could think of worse, but sure."

"But that kind of arguing is a statement of love."

"Is it?"

"We often quarrel as a way of showing our love. Otherwise, people ignore one another."

"As Théophile did with me."

"Yes," Nicolas said. "Exactly."

"I presume he has left?"

"I never saw him. I suspect he did not come to the funeral after all."

I thought about that, as we moved toward the hotel, walking side by side.

"Thank you for everything, Nicolas. Since first waking up in your apartment – well, despite that dust up with Marigold, it has seemed like paradise, so sheltered."

"It is my pleasure."

"I know you carried me to the nursing station that night. You didn't hurt your back did you?"

"No. My back is strong, and it was nice to carry you."

"I felt like a Gothic heroine in the arms of a manly man."

"Ah, take care. They were quite possessive, those Gothic heroes," he said.

"Were they now?"

"Yes. Gothic heroines were possessions, as were all women in those days; perhaps the difference is that Gothic heroines *wanted* to be possessed."

"As do I," I said quietly, because it felt true. Perhaps not possessed, but held in a protective masculine – well, hell, I'm broken as all Hell, so for the time being: possessed like a lap dog."

Nicolas laughed and kissed my cheek.

"I'm glad that you carried me down the hall, Nicolas. We Gothic heroines may be possessions, but we're picky about who carries us during a panic attack."

A view of the fields opened up through the woods, darkness quickly swallowing everything in greyish mauve haze. Standing next to Nicolas, I now found it hard to discern much except the waning glow of his shirt. Together we observed the murky beauty of the English countryside, floating toward the nearly invisible horizon, shimmering in the almost darkness like a painting.

"Nicolas?"

"Yes?"

"Are you holding my hand? Again?"

"Yes."

"That's twice today. I'm flattered. Your hand is really strong."

"The racket-ball." He gave my hand a hard squeeze.

"Wow." Then after a sensual pause. "It feels protective. I feel protected."

"I like protecting you."

"As in carrying me down hospital corridors?" I tried to look at him more clearly, but only saw his profile, a handsome French silhouette against a moonlit English landscape. Releasing his hand, I said. "This is the best I've felt since – well, since my mother died. Thank you."

"*Je t'en prie,*" Nicolas said, his voice sounding huskier.

I peeked into the hotel lounge bar. Hamish sat at a table with a glass of white wine. Going over to him, I asked, "Are you permitted to talk to me?"

"Of course," he said, sipping the wine. "However, I don't really feel like talking – to anyone. Javier gave up on me and went upstairs."

I gestured. "May I – anyway?"

"Yes."

I sat at the table and signalled to the waiter to bring me a glass of the same wine. "Why *are* you sitting in here drinking?"

"Why did you look for me here?"

"How do you know I wasn't looking for Nicolas?"

"Because he's still off chatting to people at the reception."

Since I knew this not to be true, I merely shrugged.

The waiter brought my wine. "The funeral was odd," I said.

Hamish stared into his wine. "In what way?"

"Sitting next to your Aunt Victoria Carlyle, for starters. Twelve years of so-called friendship and you never once mentioned that one of the most famous and beautiful women in the world – and *my idol* – was your Aunt? No proffered introductions? No titbits of gossip? No hints of recognition. Nothing. What the Hell else don't I know? Or is the list simply too long to recount?"

Hamish stared into his wine.

"You always had the better of me, Ham, no matter what I thought. I was the stoner Californian who got into Princeton by dint of my brains, and the rest of you, Campbell included, never saw me as anything other than a witty houseguest, a convenient handsome friend, or a good fuck."

"Thank you for taking care of Marigold this morning," Hamish said. "I imagine my dad thought everything was smooth sailing after Marigold's *Annie Get Your Gun* performance."

The waiter brought my wine, and I drank some. "*Blech.* What the Fuck is this stuff?"

"I have no idea. I just pointed at a bottle."

"Is it dessert wine? It's hideously sweet," I said

"Then don't drink it. Order something else."

I took another sip anyway. "So many veils were stripped off today; so many emperors pranced around without any clothes. A most wicked disturbance in the force. I expected Donald Trump to show up with his comb over, pot belly, ginormous booty, spouting conspiracy theories and demanding a Big Mac and fries – isn't it true he has them brought over to the White House to make sure he isn't being poisoned? As if MacDonald's employees in D.C. love him all to pieces?"

"Campbell's eulogy was nice," Hamish said. "Articulate, at any rate – which is not true of Lady what's-her-name, mother's childhood friend. Do you think she forgot to put her false teeth in or was she drunk?"

"Lady Finchampstead. Nicolas thought perhaps she was having a stroke."

"Poor thing. Hard to believe she's the same age as mom. Uncle Nathaniel did well with the reception, the house looked great."

"Unfortunately, Nicolas and I got stuck in the middle of the Scandinavian contingent for far too long. They were more intent on pitching novels for translation than mourning."

"Oh, yes, the Danish cousins. So, no takers on getting laid?"

"The last thing I want to do at the moment is get laid. The last few years have been – well, we both know what they've been. I'm taking care of myself, and just that, and then – you know, I'd like to fall in love, if and when, and all that romantic stuff. I don't think I've ever really fallen in love, not properly at any rate. I fell in fervent lust with Campbell at a time in my life when I needed – " I fell silent, my thoughts whirling wickedly. I knew not to pursue the subject further and I no longer wished to share confidences with Hamish. I gulped the ghastly wine.

We stared at one another for a long while.

"Marigold told me you said you were through with my family, that all of us could fuck off – or something to that effect."

"I *am* done with your family, and especially with you, Ham; but Marigold doth lie like a rug. I returned her angels to her, by the way, all except for Gloria Swanson. I'm keeping Gloria Swanson. Gloria had chutzpah. I have complete clarity where my argument with Marigold is concerned. It went something like this: I told her that I loved India, and that if I'd had a mother, I guess it had been her, to which Marigold responded with the delightful riposte, 'What shit. All you've ever done is take advantage of her, of us – Campbell – our family. *Fuck you, Justin.*' The last part is word-for-word correct." I paused, gauging his emotions. "I do believe the ensuing argument ended with me telling her and all of you to fuck off, but only as a logical conclusion to a stunning Trump-style potty-mouthed take-down – except she did have the balls to say it all in person and not via Twitter."

We had known one another for twelve years; I knew when Hamish believed me.

"Did you really think the funeral was odd?" he asked me.

"Yes. Perhaps not if you focus on the eloquent eulogy from the wayward child for whom your mother bought towels and ignore the morning's shotgun set-up and the rambling insensitivities from Victoria Carlyle, which rather felt like water running uphill." I drank the last of the wine. "That stuff's not so bad once you get past the first few gulps. I don't know why it was odd. But it was. There was a disturbance in the force."

"You're referencing *Star Wars*?" Hamish said.

"I'm referencing *Star Wars*."

He finished his wine and pushed his glass into the centre of the table. "I don't think that the funeral for a great artist with a terminal brain tumour, who had a heart attack in a Paris crosswalk could be anything *other* than strange in its dynamic – an unravelling of, what? Many, many things. Do you?"

I shook my head at the waiter who started toward our table. "Agreed. A total disturbance in the force. I'll miss you, Ham. But we'll be better off without one another."

"Maybe." He put his hand on top of mine. "Maybe not. Please get better. Then please do something real with your life. You're so intelligent, so clever, so creative."

"Something *real*? I don't like the sound of that at all. Reality is such a bitch. And anyway, you're supposed to say, 'may the force be with you.'"

"That *is* what I'm saying."

I looked down at our hands, stacked together on the top of the table. Our friendship ought to have ended with operatic flourish, which is how a twelve-year gay friendship *should* end: coloratura wit, heaving sobs, drunken reminiscences of Princetonian frolics. However, T. S. Elliot would have approved, inasmuch as it ended with a whimper not a bang. Twelve years of – well, at least something meaningful. Shared secrets? On my part only, it now appeared. Daily conversations then, our quotidian rendezvous with booze and boys. Hamish had been best man at my wedding. He helped me select the cake and flowers and endure the obligatory propinquity of Théophile's meddlesome mother. In any event, whimperingly it ended. No big-boned diva sang a venomous bang of a conclusion.

I regret that.

"I'm not sure that what I've done with my life thus far counts as *un*real," I said, "but I believe you're talking about my ways with men. So, how about we cut a deal? I try my best to start fresh or – reboot, perhaps. Yes, I like reboot better. And you try to grow a backbone."

"Enjoy your rebooting," he said, standing up. "There's a worried Nicolas over there, far side of the bar – eyeing us up something fierce. He's ever so caring, that man. Now," he glanced toward the door, where Javier stood watching, "My own protective man is nigh, and I *am* going to be a wild child and go get laid."

On such a warm evening, I left my window open, naked on top of the duvet, savouring the breeze. The light remained on because I had been trying to read. I had trouble concentrating, and the novel I bought for the trip proved too demanding; I kept losing the thread of the plot. About to turn the light out, I heard a tapping on the connecting door to Nicolas' room.

"Nicolas?"

The door opened and Nicolas's face peered around. "I saw that your light was remaining on."

"I can't sleep. Come in, if you want," I said, slipping under the edge of the duvet.

Nicolas entered the room wearing only his pajama bottoms, a pair of American-style boxers hairy-chested and with dark five o'clock shadow – like a Campbell meets Javier fusion. He seemed to hover, as if he wanted something.

"What is it?" I asked.

"I want you," he said, sitting without being asked on the edge of the bed. The light caught his blue eyes and made them sparkle.

"To –"

"To?"

"I mean, what is it you want me to do, Nicolas?"

Nicolas put his hand on my arm and leaned over me, saying. "You misunderstand." He brought his handsome shadowed face down and rather nervously kissed my lips. His hand, resting now on my chest, sweated. "I want you, Justin. I have wanted you for a very long time." He moved so that he could lift the duvet away from me, which he did, and then he covered me with his body. I sighed at the astonishing sensation of him, the unexpectedly wonderful feeling of his chest against mine and his rough unshaved cheek that nuzzled my neck. I lifted up his face, so that we could look at one another.

"I would like to have you, Justin, if you will let me."

I had always wanted to do it and tonight I did.

I stripped down naked, (though I kept my phone and earbuds), opened the French doors in the hotel dining room and ran across the grass, and then through the leafy, big-mansion streets of Beaconsfield. At first, I felt liberated, freed in a fashion I had only ever imagined. However, having to watch out for icky things and canine perils proved an occasional nuisance.

As I ran naked through the streets of Beaconsfield, listening to Christine and the Queens sing my favourite song,

"*Tilted*," I started crying as I thought about – too many things to hold in one blizzard of tears. I recalled how, at the age of fourteen, after my first full week of Ninth Grade, I had sat outside considering the week just past. We had eaten dinner at my richer cousin's house (a virtually identical 1930s Beverly Hills house surrounded by virtually identical Sycamore trees, one street behind our own). My independent-school educated cousin had a snappy Great Gatsby vocabulary and a trajectory to the top of American society mapped out by hired class-room hands and behind-the scenes heavy lifting. My cousin had gone to a chic Episcopal day school, and then to one of the best independent schools in Los Angeles.

My own parents thought private schooling worthlessly snobby, though not the time-saving support of a Honduran au pair, without understanding that in America *only* snobby people, crooks, cheats, braggarts and delusional orange-coloured liars with big butts actually get ahead in life – they proudly sent their only son to Beverly Hill's public schools, where I ended up in a high school that bragged that 89.4% of the students graduated. No one knew what the .4% stood for until I explained – at least to those in my homeroom – that it was merely a mathematical average and not a real number at all – for all the Board of Education knew 100% graduated last year and 25% this year. My classmates did not applaud my explanation. That night, sitting outside my cousin's house at the age of fourteen, I felt walloped; because what I learned that night was existential; it altered my life; it led directly to Princeton and Hamish, Campbell, Théophile and the rest of the weird Baz Luhrmann film I called my life.

That night I understood that, unlike my cousin with his sassy-classy uniform, Lacrosse stick, glossy new editions of classic novels, and state of the art science labs, as a public-school child, wearing my *nouveau riche* street clothes, I and my fellow students were a litter of piglets wallowing in pedagogical mud. Even if I aced every Honours and AP Course (which I did), took at least two languages (which I also did), and – *well* – got an A in everything (which I did), I would still not possess a diploma that rivalled that of my cousin. Yes, it got me into Princeton, but it took extra leaping through extra hoops. At one point in the maddening process I actually coveted that "geographic diversity" quota and wished I could be from Montana or fill in the SAT bubbles saying that I was a Mung tribesman or crippled Ukrainian orphan; when I got deferred at Harvard I thought my prospects were toast. As my chipper advisor in her pant suit told me, "No worries, you're a snap for Rice," my safety school, and seeing my scowl said, "There's nothing wrong with Rice." A long glaring look of animosity before I said, "Until you have to acknowledge that it's located in *Texas.*"

I had also looked at my cousin's 'Program of Study' that evening, which had thoroughly irked me, with its mouth-watering electives (as if his seasonal two-outfit uniform had not already made me seethe with envy). I also overheard my aunt talking about my cousin's once-a-year fancy pants school trips to Europe – famously coordinated by an ex-hippy who lived at Venice Beach and gave the students 'free time,' which she imagined they would put to good use going back to museums they had enjoyed, but simply meant drunken carousing – from Ninth Grade in St. Petersburg to Rome to London and then senior year in Paris. I would be lucky to get a spot on our February school trip to Quebec City, at the height of winter. Quebec being to winter as Tucson is to summer.

Of course, even as a child, I never looked mussed. *I* should have had the crisp uniform and mandatory dress shoes.

In summer, flies landed on my cousin by the – whatever you called a herd of flies – but not on me. In spring, my shoes never muddied. My bicycle remained as clean after ten years of use as the day my grandparents bought it for me. At school, my homework invariably came in the neatest. I easily won every debate championship; I had been the stalwart lead in *The Pirates of Penzance*. So, realizing that I had come through the fires of my life and now had to make sense of what remained of Justin Abernathy, I ran naked through the streets of Beaconsfield, listening to Christine and the Queens, cursing my cousin, my parents, Théophile, terrorists, roof-slate installers, and crying my eyes out, suddenly screaming, "*I fucking hate all of the fucking goddamned world except for Nicolas*," and crying all the harder and screaming all the louder as lights popped on in bedroom windows.

No one had made love to me with the ardour and passion of Nicolas. He loved me. Considering we had known one another long enough for every character flaw to be well documented, it felt – how did it feel? It awoke something in me. Maybe I had loved Nicolas too? Certainly, his kisses felt right, our sex felt loving, and resting in his arms made me feel strangely happy. I had no fear that he would leave. My safety seemed sure. Théophile and I had bonded over the search for Didier and Benôit, his dutiful help that night made us closer than ever we had been. He had been his nicest self in those days after the Bâtaclan. But we had never fused in the way Nicolas and I tonight. I'd lived in France long enough to see the romantic ideal – *fusionnel* – when it ravished me. I paused, looked up at the quickening sky, and realized that I could not remember in which language Nicolas and I had expressed our love.

And then, I had to climb back up into my room via an oak tree, since someone had picked up my clothes and locked the dining room doors. At least I had the rest of the night to think up a plausible excuse for losing my clothes, which, curled up in the arms of warm, furry, sleeping Nicolas, I did.

I awoke with Nicolas's breath against my neck, curled within his embrace, my back to his chest. Early morning light came through the window. It fell across the foot of the bed. I stared open-eyed into the shadowed room. As if born to a lover's shielding posture, Nicolas' left arm came around me possessively. His right arm had disappeared somewhere beneath the pillow. For the first time since mother's beheading and the deaths of Didier and Benôit, I had slept through the night without a nightmare (or at least one that I could remember).

"You are awake," Nicolas said.

"Yes." I pulled his arm more tightly about my chest, clinging to it.

He kissed the back of my neck, saying, "Holding you in my arms like this is – " but he seemed to lack the words, and merely buried his face in my shoulder.

I pulled his arm even more snugly about me.

9

I sat by a window in the library sipping a cup of coffee, waiting for Nicolas.

Victoria Carlyle's voice so caught me off guard that I sloshed coffee on the Wilton carpet. "I like your handsome hunk of a boyfriend," she said. "When I arranged for the two of you to sit beside me, I had no idea I was dialling up such a delectable couple."

"He is delectable, I agree."

"A thoughtful lad from what I could tell," she said, sitting beside me in an ornate Queen Anne chair, a soft scent of lavender wafting outward. "He's quite manly, I should think, knowing a bit about these things myself. Clearly, we both like them hot and hairy. Nathaniel was just so when I married him, and though he's still hairy, it's gone rather grey and ratty, and he is definitely not hot – unless you like middle-aged men who sag everywhere."

At a loss for words, I stared at the woman who had been my heroine, then someone rather horrid yesterday at the funeral, and now someone fragrantly feminine, though borderline outrageous.

She gestured out the window toward the garden. "You know, Justin, India told me many times that she lived her life vicariously through you and that you really were like a son to her. Occasionally, our conversations seemed only to be about you. Apparently, she compiled your witticisms, which seems silly to me, but India was like that, unfortunately. At any rate, she clearly thought of you as one of her own – and at least you didn't shoot up the church and then flee back to Australia or unbutton your shirt at the reception on the pretext that it was too warm, as Campbell did, in the hopes of shagging a cater waiter, I presume." She sighed. "Perhaps you were her favourite."

"Well, that's not how things ended between us. Our last conversation was a nightmare. She endorsed the family's demand for my separation from Hamish – you know, the idea that I was a bad influence, that I somehow inhibited him or stunted his growth."

"I don't believe the two things are incompatible. Do you? India loved you. And you *have* been a bad influence on Hamish, but much of that is Hamish's fault. He's susceptible to influences. Javier will run that household with an iron fist. My advice is to accept that India loved your vitality, your laughter and naughtiness, and just let go of Hamish and see what happens. Perhaps he'll come yoyo-ing back. His type often does."

I looked out the window at the rose garden.

"I'm beginning to crave one of those old-fashioned English breakfasts," she said, "with fried everythings: tomatoes, mushrooms, sausages, eggs, ham. I never eat such dreck in London, but whenever I'm in the countryside with American tourists, I tend to go a bit wild."

I looked at her, this famous woman whom I had long ago placed on a pedestal. "You *arranged* for Nicolas and me to sit by you?"

"Quite."

"May I ask why?"

"You may." She smiled. "I was sizing you up, seeing if India had been accurate. I'm looking for an editor for my new Paris office, someone fresh, someone witty, someone stylish."

I looked at her with a full-on blush.

She laughed. "You have a B.A. in English, Magna cum laude, with a minor in Journalism, from Princeton no less; you're fluent in French and, rather fortuitously, you live in Paris and have a *Titre de Séjour* that allows you to work. *Voilà.*"

"But I've never done anything even remotely like being an editor. I'm a school administrator."

"At one of the fanciest lycées in France, which must demand the negotiating skills of Talleyrand." She pretended to shiver. "I should think you would consider this your chance to escape. A thirtieth birthday present. Of course, I'm an ogre to work for, that goes without saying, but one adapts. So, are you interested or not, young man?"

I watched her for a moment or two. "You know that I have PTSD, with an embarrassing proclivity for panic attacks."

"All the best editors have bats in their belfries," she said. "With time, the edge will wear off, people will adjust to your panic – or not. And you will become someone new; you will feel like someone new."

Her words resonated. "Oddly, long before my mother's decapitation and my friends' slaughter, I wanted to be someone else. I didn't quite fit in my life. I imagined different things. At one point, I thought I had found myself in India's family, with Hamish, Campbell and Marigold."

"*Pooh*," she said, with a contemptuous wave of her hand. "Rather like the hare-brained characters from Wodehouse or Mitford, that family." She looked at me with scrutinizing concentration. "Look at you: Handsome, sexy, witty. Yes, and well you know it. Envious eyes have followed you, young man. You have everything others want – well, except athletic prowess and mechanical aptitude. But beauty, wit and style beat mechanical aptitude any day."

I couldn't help but smile; in fact, I nearly laughed.

"Do you still hate theme parks? India once told me that you hated theme parks. I should be clear that I approve."

"Hate is not the word I would use to describe my feelings for them. Loathe, detest, repulsed by – there are hundreds of options. Why? Something about a funeral and my confession that my life has felt like an empty mess makes you think of theme parks? Okay," I said, as if having reflected on it, "I understand that." I looked at her. "Why *are* you asking me about theme parks?"

"Just gauging where the Justin barometer is – or where it is not."

"Where theme parks are concerned, it remains the same."

"I could do with a glass of champagne," Victoria said.

"To forget about theme parks and other tragedies?"

"Yes. And to celebrate my new Paris editor." Her face seemed serious all of a sudden. "You're free now, Justin – the door is open, and you can either sit where horror placed you or fly right out through the open door. You're free."

Epilogue

Victoria's limo glided to a stop, someone opened the door for us and she took the proffered hand. I followed behind. In we went and up a flight of stairs to a dressing room, with roses, toast points, caviar, and bottles of Badoit mineral water, the things her staff would have demanded. She snappishly asked for some Tisane, preferably Jasmine – merely to make a point. Someone scrambled off in confusion. A director babbled at her, a make-up person blotted and wiped. Eyes observed her, like Marie Antoinette on her way to the guillotine, I thought. Someone else showed her an outline, but she handed it to me; not bothering even to glance at it. Then, someone else took her arm and led us into a larger room with several robotic cameras, like cyborgs, stuffed chairs, and a backdrop meant to resemble an Italian villa. I lurked by one of the friendlier-looking Cyborgs. The painted view resembled a villa on Capri in which Théophile and I once stayed: it had an uncanny resemblance. I almost heard again the intruding sounds of tourists on the rocks below.

Her interviewer hurried in, all perky warmth, which I saw startled Victoria. Had she expected New York *sang-froid*? They shook hands. The interviewer chattered away about something in the morning papers, which merely baffled Victoria, since she – like most Europeans – chose to ignore the antics of the country's infantile, obese President and his court of sycophants, crooks and cronies (including those who weren't family members). The interviewer asked Victoria if she minded talking about her extended family.

"Honestly?" Victoria asked, as if their subject at hand might really be avoided.

"What counts as honesty these days?" the interviewer asked, "*Fake news*," she roared, in a mocking Presidential voice.

They both laughed.

"We'll be recording this," she reminded Victoria, "it's not really live. It can be edited – *if necessary.*"

"I attended Marlborough," Victoria said, "I doubt it will need to be edited."

For a moment the interviewer seemed baffled, then, "Right. Are you ready?"

"Indeed. Since I arrived," Victoria said.

"Maybe we could start with your signature smile?"

Victoria smiled at the camera.

"That's it," she said. "Some smile."

"Practice makes perfect."

The interviewer leaned forward. "Your parents. Famous. The Chattertons. Wealthy. Powerful. Their names opened doors."

"Whether I wanted them open or not."

"Excuse me?" The interviewer asked in apparent confusion

"People tried to please my family, even when we just wanted to do a little shopping like anyone else." She flashed her Victoria smile again.

"But you have to admit, your family has mythic proportions – Members of Parliament, an OBE, Boards of Directors, well – the list would be endless."

Again, they both laughed.

"Your sister's death?" the interviewer said. "It must still affect you."

"Sudden death is hard to come to grips with. If she had a weak heart, no one knew it, I doubt she knew it. She'd been troubled and had been taking medication for her brain tumour, but no one has yet to indicate a link."

"When you heard about it, you must have been – ?"

"Distraught. However, the French were magnificent about keeping us informed."

"Your Paris editor, whom you have described as, 'Like a son to you,' has found himself tossed about in the tabloid press. Care to speak about that?" She seemed not to realize that I made nice with my sexy Cyborg friend not ten feet from her.

"Well, why not," Victoria said, with a flicker's glance at me.

"He has fallen in love with a French aristocrat. One reads that you and your husband are planning an enormous wedding for them."

"*Enormous?* Depends on one's perspective. Perhaps the reception shall be enormous. Actually, it's a beautiful story of love and caring, and he couldn't have chosen a more marvellous husband. In fact, I first met them both together, at my sister's funeral. A delightful tale of romance. He started out as my assistant before we became like mother and son, and his husband is indeed from a revered French family."

"But don't you agree that it's a most *unusual* story?" the interviewer asked, keeping them on task.

"Unusual? Yes. I suppose. In certain aspects." Victoria said disingenuously.

"Certain aspects," the interviewer hedged, "Wouldn't you like to talk about your gay French editor with PTSD? About his mother's peculiar death when she was decapitated by a roof slate? His sister on a farm in Hawaii with a white supremacist? About his aristocratic fiancé?"

Victoria looked at her interviewer for an unguarded instant as if she were a moron.

"Discussing the wonderful peculiarities of my Paris Editor's life on television doesn't quite feel like something well-bred people do."

"You agreed to appear this morning." The interviewer seemed puzzled.

"Yes, because I'm the Editor of *Sense and Sensibility* and I'm in New York and you invited me."

"We did, for sure, and thanks so much. Well, comes a time one must make a statement – a public acknowledgement. Don't you think?"

Victoria took a deep breath, trying to keep her signature smile glued to her face. "Difficult to acknowledge what is already public knowledge, but I am happy to say that I am happy." She almost appeared to add, '… that I am happy to say.' She sighed. "One has no control over one's sister's Nazi inclinations, as I'm sure many would attest over the years. Didn't Soviet Youth children actually turn in their parents? I mean -- really? But why on earth is that relevant? To anything? I read that your father belongs to the NRA and accidentally shot your brother at a hunt in North Carolina. What does one hunt in North Carolina? One's relatives?" My Cyborg and I thought the interview had started to resemble the Mad Hatter's Tea Party – I felt empathetic mechanical twitchings from my friend.

"What about what they've said about you?" interviewer woman asked.

"I'm not sure to what you refer, but as the female editor of the world's top fashion magazine what's been said about me would rival the best of them. However, that's where I stay above the fray. I'm not going to talk about myself *per se*."

"Your niece shot the crotches off of statuary at your sister's funeral, your sister-in-law Elizabeth died soon after and her novel of lesbian love, which she had kept hidden for many years, has soared to number one in the United Kingdom – and now your Paris editor with an – shall we say eccentric life, is marrying a French aristocrat. You must admit it's quite the story."

"I *must* admit nothing. My family is delightfully eccentric. It's something I understand. Now, our New York, London and Paris editions of my magazine have marvellous editions this month – and the story in them is not my sister-in-law's brilliant lesbian novel or shooting gallery theatrics in historic churches, but rather the new fall fashions." Victoria kept smiling though I knew she inwardly cursed; I also knew she couldn't leave well enough alone. She couldn't. "Why should the public care about my sister-in-law camping rough in the Lake District and hiking – oh, whatever mountain that was. I mean, *really*. I'm sure she was an enchanting lesbian. As to my niece's reckless shotgun practice upon apparently costly statuary, I can only say that grief, alcohol and maternal longing for her five youngsters in the antipodes did not mix well. I accept that my Editor's wedding will be news – but I'd hardly call it the wedding of the decade as some have done, though he would love it if I did." Again, the practiced smile and another flicker in my direction. I could have sworn the cyborg nudged me, but no doubt it merely adjusted a camera angle.

"I sense that you dislike the fact that your life is public domain."

"Often. Yes."

"Your family is famous."

"Ah, but we did not choose fame. We are not the Kardashnahoonians." With a noticeable sigh, Victoria took a look at the phony Italian villa, and the make-believe view from a make-believe window, and I saw her thinking through her smile, 'The things I bloody well do for my family.' She and the interviewer looked at one another. "A very handsome and I dare say delectable French aristocrat, who was the star of his renowned Lycee's handball team, is marrying my clever, handsome and soon-to-be-famous Paris Editor," Victoria said, family pride having made her decide to give this pretty interviewer a kick in the crotch with an all-American fairy tale. "In fact, I think anyone would simply *love* welcoming into their extended family a man as tall, handsome, broad-shouldered, big-chested and heroic as Nicolas Perrault. Of course, they will *not* be ordering their wedding cake from those Hillbilly bakers in Colorado, endorsed by your Supreme Court for their bigotry."

I had been quickly texting Nicolas, "*U played Hball at Lycée???*"

His answer pinged backed. "*Louis-le-Grand has never heard of sports. What????*"

After a moment of vaguely befuddled pause, Victoria's interviewer said. "Thank you."

"No," Victoria said, "Thank *you.*"

I noticed that someone had cleverly given all of the Cyborgs playful name tags: Denzel Washington, Rudolph Valentino, Hallie Berry. I searched for the name of mine, expecting something butch. A brain-electrifying shock: Gloria Swanson. I flushed; she nudged me again. Victoria Carlyle winked at me. Nicolas texted. "*MDR. Can't stop laughing. Hball at Ls-le-Grand!*"

"Oh – well, of course, I mean – " the interviewer stammered.

Victoria smiled that famous smile, and said in French, "*On peut se jester dans la guele du loup.*" And then in English, "And survive."

About the Author

Mark Albro has studied and worked in Paris, where he currently lives. He is a scholar of French fiction and has written for European academic publications. The son of a psychologist, Mark imagined he had better coping skills than most for the tragedy of the Bataclân terrorist attack on the night of November 13, 2015. He did not. His and his friends' struggles to come to grips with that event now demarcate his life. Living on the street where Rimbaud came of age and dining where Hemingway's Jake Barnes rode away from Montparnasse with Lady Brett Ashley, Mark agrees (and Keeping Gloria Swanson proves) that Paris is still a movable feast.

www.ingramcontent.com/pod-product-compliance
Lightning Source LLC
Chambersburg PA
CBHW020018030726
47499CB00007B/2170